Sabotage!

Jason was in his fighter craft, slamming his ship through the openings among the spinning asteroids. His nine classmates were spread out behind him and to the sides. He could not see the fox they chased, the decoy ship, but it had left a faint trail of ionized hydrogen that his scanners tracked, lost, and tracked onto again.

There — behind a planetoid — his scanners caught a hint of the fox! Almost undetectable — he'd better verify it before bursting around the planetoid; the turn and braking on the fox's side would be tricky. Jason slammed on his rets.

They did not respond. He knew what was about to happen. That brief instant imprinted itself on his mind — his ship plummeting for the dark surface of the planetoid, back-up systems dead, alarms and his own voice screaming in his ears, and the calm thought behind it all, I am about to die.

OMNI
ASTROPILOTS

LAURA J. MIXON

SCHOLASTIC INC.
New York Toronto London Auckland Sydney

This book is dedicated, with love,
to my niece,
Stephanie Sheree Maez.

No part of this publication may be reproduced in whole or in part, or stored in a retrieval system, or transmitted in any form or by any means, electronic, mechanical, photocopying, recording, or otherwise, without written permission of the publisher. For information regarding permission, write to Scholastic Inc., 730 Broadway, New York, NY 10003.

ISBN 0-590-40277-3

Copyright © 1987 by Omni Publications International Ltd. & Laura J. Mixon. All rights reserved. Published by Scholastic Inc.

Omni is a registered trademark of Omni Publications International, Ltd.

12 11 10 9 8 7 6 5 4 3 2 1   7 8 9/8 0 1 2/9

Printed in the U.S.A.   01

First Scholastic printing, June 1987

Chapter 1

Andrea Ito sat down at the library computer console, dumped the contents of her satchel onto the table, and sorted through the laser-traced fax sheets and the data lattices. She riffled through the lattice cards and put one into the depression above the keyboard. Then she booted the software, folded her long legs beneath her, and settled down to study.

For the past four years her instructors had tried to break her of that habit — without success. Andrea was simply uncomfortable sitting with her back straight and feet flat on the floor and would only do so under extreme duress, such as the threat of expulsion from Collegium.

It was a threat the school administrators seldom used after her first test results were in. Collegium was not a military school, not exactly, and a casual posture was hardly an infraction of the rules. But there was, after all, such a thing as decorum. Not to mention the reputation of Collegium, a reputation Andrea was stubborn about neglecting. At least when it came to her posture while seated.

Andrea simply ignored unimportant and irrelevant warnings of this sort.

Some time later, she looked over the top of her carrel. The library was filling with students; it must be later than she had thought. Andrea was the duty officer today, but she had hoped to do a little studying for her final before she went to work.

I'd better quit messing around and find out what I have to do, she thought. She cleared her computer screen and called up the duty roster. Andrea read her duties and groaned. "Harvest time" again. She would have to test and evaluate all the candidates for admission, then choose, or "harvest," the best. The test results were then to be reported directly to Senior Admin Trammerden, more popularly known as the Hammer, though never to his face. The grunt jobs always seemed to fall on her days.

Andrea called up the stats of the candidates she was to evaluate and scanned the displays quickly. This term the harvest was a small one with only five candidates. Three of the candies were from Earth, and one was from the Lunar city, Mweri Mirembe. The fifth, surprisingly, was older, a sixteen-year-old from the faraway colony on 40 Eridani II. Few outsystem colonists had ever attended Collegium.

Commonwealth citizens, including Andrea's father, did not like Eridanians very much, because funds that would have gone to the Commonwealth's Martian, Jovian, Saturnian, and asteroid communities had instead been pumped into making 40 Eridani II livable and profitable.

Andrea had never met an outsystem colonist; she was interested in seeing what he was like.

As she collected her materials, one of her classmates, Paul Garcia y la Vega, strode over to her carrel and leaned on the console. "Are you free for second shift, Andy?"

She looked up, brushing away the hair that had strayed across her face. "Got a harvest today. A shipload of candies just arrived and I'm duty officer. Again. Sorry."

Paul grimaced sympathetically. Small and dark, he was a sixteen-year-old with a charismatic, quicksilver smile, the son of a Terran mining executive. By Collegiate standards, Paul was only a mediocre pilot, but he had an uncanny tracker's sense that made up in part for his slightly slower reflexes. Paul's weird radar had earned him the nickname Weasel, a name he pretended to loathe, though Andrea suspected he was privately pleased at this backhanded nod to his ability.

"And I thought I had it bad," he said with feeling. "I'm working in the newsfax center all afternoon. "Well," he tapped the top of the console, "if you finish early, a group of us plan to rendezvous in Rec Center 5j at eighteen 'oh. If you feel like chilling down with us."

"I'll try." Andrea glanced at her chronometer and gasped. "I'm late for the harvest. See you."

She unfolded herself from the chair, dashed through the library aisles and carrels, and

forced her way through the door before its
energy barrier had time to dissolve completely.
She hurried down the curving corridor at her
fastest walk; it would not do to break into a
frantic run before all the younger students
going to class.

Andrea finally halted before the entry to the
Pit (Pre-Indoctrination Test Facility, as the
mints, the school administrators, called it),
took a deep breath, and smoothed her flight
jacket while the door's field faded from violet,
through the visible spectrum, to transparence.
Then she stepped inside.

Technicians were already issuing white cotton
gowns to the five candidates who stood in the
antechamber's center. Beyond an open arch
were the implements of torture: the machines
that would determine whether the candidates
were Collegiate material. Andrea called their
names to mind and tried to match the stats to
the faces.

The Eridanian, Jason Stiletto, was easy; he
was dressed in leather boots, high-waisted
pants, and a billowing shirt. No one insystem
dressed like that. Several years older than the
other candidates, he had a thin face harshened
with crags, a large, patrician nose, a square
jaw, and full lips.

His stats said he was sixteen, but to Andrea
he looked older. Compact, slim, standing
straight as a knife blade, he returned her
appraisal with an arrogant, emerald-eyed stare.

Andrea frowned slightly. Great. Not only was
he too old to be a recruit, he had a chip on his

shoulder the size of Titan. A definite no, she decided.

The other four were between the ages of eleven and fourteen. The Loonie was probably the blonde girl next to the Eridanian; she appeared weary and sluggish. A Lunar citizen would have difficulty adjusting to Collegium's heavier gravity, which ranged from 1.2 gees at the center to 0.6 gees in the outer modules. The other three were from Earth, two redheaded brothers from Eastern Europe and an Ethiopian girl.

While she studied the candidates, Andrea stood at ease: feet planted shoulder-length apart, left wrist clasped in right hand behind her back. All but the Eridanian were fidgeting, eyeing her nervously. The youngest of them, the Loonie girl, appeared close to tears.

"I am Andrea Ito," she told them. "Senior Colleague Pilot, Class of 2106. That's what these arrows mean," she gestured at the two inverted silver chevrons on her left chest, "that I'm a pilot. All five of you have stats that indicate you might be," she stressed the qualifier, "Collegiate material." She approached the candidates and strolled past them, looking them up and down. "That's what we're here to find out."

Only the Eridanian had the nerve to look her in the eye. Andrea stopped and stared coolly at him until he looked away. Then she assumed her former position, facing all five.

She recognized the look in their eyes, the mingled hope and apprehension. Four years before, a tall, gangly, twelve-year-old Andrea, along with her best friend Teresa and nine others, had stood barefoot in a knee-length white gown before a senior pilot who ran through the initial speech in a bored tone.

Every time she did a harvest the memory returned in sharp detail: the excitement Teresa and she had shared, the heady plans they had made, the sudden terror, her longing to return home to Forty League About, the submarine city that moved through the heated oceans beneath Europa's icy crust.

Andrea had been one of the lucky few to be accepted, not only as a student, but as a pilot, too. Teresa had not been accepted at all. Their friendship had ended, violently, that same night. A year later Andrea had returned to Forty Leagues About to learn that all her old friendships had evaporated like dry ice. Still, she had no regrets. But harvests were a painful reminder of that loss; she did not enjoy overseeing them.

Andrea looked up at the ceiling while she spoke. "Out of the ten-thousandth of one percent of the population of humanity that has the skills needed to attend a space-tech academy," she informed them, "only one in another thousand has what it takes to make it into Collegium as a dreg . . . a freshman.

"Collegium is unique," she said. "It's the only space-tech school in the asteroid belt, and the only one that is truly politically neutral. None of the Earth nations, nor the corporations, have any claim on Collegium. We make no distinction here between Terrans and non-Terrans. That's the first lesson you learn here, and you'd better learn it quickly.

"We already know you are smart enough to study here." She paused again and looked at them. "Intelligence is not the only factor that determines whether you'll be able to work effectively, for long periods of time, in space or on alien worlds. The tests we will perform on you today will measure other qualities, such as your quickness, coordination, response to crises, and emotional stability. This means," she went on casually, "that if you pass the tests, and make it through the curriculum, and don't break any of Collegium's rules, you will be literally one in a billion. *If* you make it."

She noted that the Eridanian looked at her with mild cynicism. She added, gazing directly at him, "And, by the way, the surest way to get kicked out of Collegium is to act like you know everything and walk around with a chip on your shoulder. With that kind of attitude it's highly unlikely that you'll last six weeks here. Or even six hours." Then she looked at her chronometer and gestured to the techs. "Let's get started."

After the candidates had changed into their cotton gowns, the techs led them over to a row of tables and wired them up to the physiological monitors. The fizz test was about to begin.

Andrea watched as the techs applied electrodes to the candidates' scalps, upper arms, torsos, and legs; they were all fitted with dream specs that covered their eyes and ears and made them look like insects. The specs blotted out all sound and vision, so that dream shows could be run in the candies' minds and their autonomic responses measured. She glanced at the Eridanian; his expression was impassive. She frowned. No candy should be that calm.

Jason "Stiletto" was a good deal more unusual than Andrea Ito would ever have suspected. His outsystem citizenship and calm demeanor were the least amazing things about him.

And in spite of his appearance, he was quite uncomfortable. This was the test he had most feared. His breathing was loud within the helmet. The dream spec's inner pads pressed against his cheekbones and chin; in the crevices between the pads, cold beads of sweat crawled down his face.

Stay chill, MacLeod, he thought. It's not the real fizz test, only a low-level stress stimulus for gauging untrained candidates. I've already had four years of training here that they don't know about. I won't break. I don't twitch out under mild stress.

He forced his heart rate to slow. A thin, mirthless smile touched his lips. Relax, Jason, he told himself. They don't know who you are or why you're here. A little caution on your part and he will never know you're back. Until it's far too late.

Chapter 2

When the candies were all wired up, Andrea had the techs start the dream machines. She watched their responses on the consoles mounted above their heads. Amber lines snaked across the gray of the screens, peaked, and dove through fields of changing numbers. The candies began to twitch and murmur.

Andrea noted that the girl from Ethiopia was a real possibility for pilot. She had an unusually low metabolic rate, but her reaction time was outstanding, and she would probably respond to danger by taking action, rather than by freezing. The two other Terrans and the Loonie didn't look so promising. But the younger boy wasn't doing too badly. And his stats had shown that he possessed outstanding analytical skills. He wouldn't qualify as a pilot, but he might make a good engineer; if he passed the psychological and gravity gauntlet tests, Andrea would accept him as a student.

The older boy was a mummy; his read-outs indicated that he would freeze or panic in an emergency. Andrea ruled him out immediately.

Then she stopped before the Eridanian's display. "Jan." She called one of the techs over. "Is this monitor working correctly?"

The tech, a large, blonde, older woman, bent over the Eridanian to check his electrodes and monitoring system. Jason's hands were contracting almost imperceptibly, and his lips were tightly pursed as though he were afraid of what he might say while under dream stimulation.

Jan finally turned to Andrea. "It's all in order, Colleague." Then she glanced at the screen and whistled sharply. "Look at that reaction time! And his coordination, and his response to stress — practically textbook." She slapped Andrea on the shoulder with a hoot. "Looks like you hooked yourself an ace, kid."

Andrea frowned deeply at the readings. He was too old and had a rotten attitude to boot. But with a read-out like this . . . well, most likely the psych tests would eliminate him.

She did not want this outsystem hick from the Eridani colony to become a pilot. With his snotty attitude he would probably end up being a loner, a rogue, and she did not want to be the colleague who had recruited a rogue. Recruiting one could damage her career almost as badly as turning rogue herself.

Rogue. There was no worse smear of a Collegium graduate's name. Because pilots who turned rogue on their teams endangered others' lives.

Andrea stroked her chin pensively, then turned to Jan. "Give him the second-year test. I want to see where his twitch-out point is."

Jan appeared doubtful. "That's a little un-orthodox."

"Jan, no one — but no one — who is un-trained comes through the candy fizz test with-out even a waver on their stress reaction read-out. Either he had some kind of training on Eridani II or . . . I don't know what. But I'm going to find out where he breaks."

Jan shrugged her broad shoulders and turned to the machine, increasing the stress setting. Meanwhile, Andrea directed the other techs to unhook the rest of the candidates and get them started on their psych tests.

Andrea stood before the Eridanian's monitor, watching the stress line intently. She remem-bered her first run through the second-year fizz test, when she was a sophomore. She had come away with a monstrous headache and a case of the shakes that had lasted the better part of a day.

The dream machine was designed to present a series of images to the subject's subconscious and, by monitoring his or her responses, begin to stimulate dreams that caused the subject to react violently. In other words, it produced nightmares.

Jason had been riding the dreams; they had been unsettling, but so low-stress that he had remembered they were only dreams and had met no terrifying mind-dragons. Now, though, the dreams were becoming more real.

He had already relived the time he had almost drowned when he was six and was now in the midst of a memory from when he was ten, just before he left for Collegium the first time. This was the one that had caused him to twitch out when he was a real candy, back in 2084, about twenty-two years ago, stay-time.

The dream machine recreated the memory with an eerie clarity. It was April, 2068. Jason had gotten out of school only a few days before.

In three days, he would leave for Sol on an interstellar cruiser. He had done so well on his school exams that the colony's head administrator had paid his parents a visit to persuade them to send Jason to Sol, almost sixteen light-years away.

Time is respectful of light. The closer you approach the speed of light, the more time slows down. If you could travel at virtually the speed of light, time would almost freeze for you; to someone "stationary," in stay-time, you would appear motionless — trapped in amber.

But to you, traveling at virtually the speed of light, it would be as if the rest of the universe had sped up around you. You would be in dial-time. Einstein had predicted it and named it Special Relativity.

Jason's parents had been reluctant. The trip took sixteen years one-way, stay-time; if they sent him to Collegium he would not be back for almost forty years. But it was too great an opportunity for them to decide for Jason; when they had asked him, desire awakened and blazed like a fire in his heart — to be a Collegium pilot — to control the fastest craft in the galaxy! He had insisted with such fierce tenacity that his parents had finally, and tearfully, capitulated.

So Jason was leaving. His best friend Aleyn and he had decided to do something to bind their friendship through the many years they would be apart. They had always wanted to explore the caves in the seaside cliffs, but had hesitated because the caverns were partially submerged in the toxic waters of the beautiful and deadly ocean; the caves were fully submerged at high tide. Until this day, the two boys had never dared to go beyond the entrances.

Jason and Aleyn entered the seaside caves. Aleyn led because the excursion had been his idea. Jason could see only his flashlight and the silhouette of his shoulders and head. The boys made their way through tunnels of pitted glass, carefully avoiding the pitfalls, and sinking their phosphorescent markers in the walls as they went.

And then, without even a cry, Aleyn and his light were gone. There was a splash. At Jason's feet was a deep pit. When he shone his light into the pit he saw his friend lying face down in a pool several meters below. Horror overtook him. He called Aleyn's name, began to cry — Aleyn was dead, dead! Jason was screaming, fleeing through the tunnels to get help, but they would be too late; he knew they would not make it back before high tide. . . .

No. He must not panic, or Aleyn would die. With a tremendous effort of will, he rejected the terror. He did not panic; he set pitons on the rim of the pit, then climbed down into the hole. At the bottom, he rolled Aleyn over; his friend's face was blue and bloated — he had been dead for days. Jason slammed against the wall in terror. . . .

No. It had only been moments since Aleyn had fallen. When Jason looked back, Aleyn's face was pale; he was unconscious but not dead. From the twisted angle of his leg, Jason knew it was broken. He looked upward and swallowed despair; although he was older and larger than Aleyn, it was a long way up and out. Nothing for it, he thought grimly. He strapped his unconscious friend to his back and started his long climb.

Abruptly the dream faded. Jason drew a deep breath, relieved. I can still ride the dragon, he thought. I didn't twitch.

An alien's voice whispered into his mind . . .

"Ja . . . a . . . son, are you all right? . . . I sensed fear . . . when you did not answer I grew concerned. . . ."

"All's chill, Sssrei," Jason assured his traveling companion. "This will be over soon. Are you holding out okay?"

The alien projected a disgruntled image of itself curled in Jason's luggage, its filaments furled, unable to shift position for fear of ruining Jason's clothes. "If 'okay' means miserably uncomfortable, then yes, I am okay," it told him peevishly.

Jason suppressed a quick grin. "Hang in there, Sssrei. They're testing me. It'll only be a little while longer, I promise."

"Human promises . . ." Sssrei replied with a definite acerbic edge.

When Jason's vision settled he was fourteen years old, a Collegiate senior pilot, standing in the academy's launch bay, next to his little fighter craft. He knew in horror what the dream machine had hooked into — not this one, he thought, I'm not ready to ride this one yet. But it was too late, the scene was already under way.

Tomorrow graduation exercises would start. He wanted to make one last check of his craft. The launch bay was deserted. Jason crossed confidently to his little ship. Although he was the youngest of his graduation class, he had consistently finished at the top of his class in his double major, mechanics and astrophysics, as well as in navigation, and the myriad simulations.

The last three years had been horribly difficult — but he had won the respect and admiration of his classmates and teachers and was the provisional class valedictorian, the prov-valley. A few members of his class resented and hated him, particularly Tram, a boy two years older than he.

Tram was only a fraction less adept than Jason in the exercises, and he occasionally outperformed him in classwork, especially in computer programming. Tram was good, there was no doubt of that. There was a chance that Tram might outperform him during the exercises, but Jason was determined to win.

Salutatorian was an impressive honor, too, Jason thought as he opened the panels of his ship and exposed the navigational circuitry. Finishing Collegium's curriculum at all was enough of an honor, really. But Jason wanted to be the best of the best.

He pulled out his tracer and checked the circuitry boards. The techs had already made a final check, but occasionally they missed things — Jason's thoroughness had paid off before. The circuits that controlled the back-up navigation were crucial; if he lost computer controls even for an instant he would be smeared against a planetoid in microseconds.

Everything was in order. Jason sealed the panel and stood, wiping his hands on the midnight blue of his canvas pants.

The lights flickered suddenly, and a low hum from his chronometer announced a level five alarm. He frowned, annoyed. Level five was as minor as you could get, but the mints might decide to postpone graduation exercises. He headed for the exit at a trot.

Just outside, in the corridor, he ran into Tram. The older boy looked uncharacteristically nervous; his broad, oval face was flushed, and he was out of breath. When he saw Jason, his lips stretched across his teeth in an unpleasant smile.

"Hey, MacLeod, the mints have been looking for you."

"What is it?"

"An unpredicted meteor impact on one of the shield satellites. Thompson wants you to calculate and reprogram the other satellites' positions to bring the shield network back up, until the repair crew gets out there."

Jason stifled a groan. It would be just like Tram to finagle grunt work like this for Jason, just before graduation exercises.

"It won't work, Tram," Jason said flatly. "I'll have the network repatched in a couple of hours and still slag your tail in the exercises."

Tram's gray, hawk glance was icy. "You present no threat to me, MacLeod. Don't flatter yourself that I had anything to do with this assignment. After all," he remarked as he continued toward the launch bay, "as prov-valley you're clearly the only one qualified to oversee such important work."

"Rogue trash," Jason muttered under his breath and then headed toward the hub shuttles.

Andrea clocked the Eridanian during the fizz test. For the first fifteen minutes there were only minor quivers in his stress line. He was easily compensating for the machine's effect by regaining control of the dream scenarios and completing them successfully.

She had seen the exact point that the machine found his dragon; needle pricks of adrenaline jittered across the screen; his heart rate doubled. Right now he was struggling to regain control, to ride the dragon.

Andrea wondered with a twinge of sympathy what private monsters he was viewing. To subject an untrained candidate to second-year-level nightmares was cruel and unusual; she gnawed her lip in belated indecision. Andrea could not believe he was holding out so well. His hormone levels were close to maxing out. It was not a dragon he was riding; it was a slagging *volcano*. But no, his responses were starting to stabilize. He was going to beat the machine.

Jason was in his fighter craft, slamming his ship through the openings among the spinning asteroids. His nine classmates were spread out behind him and to the sides. He could not see the fox they chased, the decoy ship, but it had left a faint trail of ionized hydrogen that his scanners tracked, lost, and tracked onto again.

Jason had made this run through the asteroid maze nicknamed the Road to Glory several times. But before the exercises, new rocks had been brought in and the maze rearranged; Jason did not want to become overconfident. His gaze flitted across the control board as he corrected and responded to the computer's decisions. He had no time for the apprehension that tried to burst from his gut. He had to stay chill, remain in control. But it was easier wished for than willed.

Suddenly, his control slipped — pain shrieked across his mind — he lay in searing agony, in his ship's wreckage — his mind reeled — not ready for this, not ready!

With effort, Jason shoved the dream aside. The feeling faded and in seconds the memory evaporated, as though it had never happened. He was again piloting his craft, no real danger if he were careful; he was approaching the fox. . . .

Dim chunks of rock, ice, and metal raced past the window of his cockpit. Jason focused all of his mind and will on the grid, the computer simulation of the planetoid maze that hung before him. Uneasiness gnawed at his stomach, drawing his attention from the chase; enemy ghost ships flickered at the periphery of his mind. Jason ignored them. They were only his fear, trying to distract him.

His concentration wavered again. Far to his right, he glanced over and saw Tram, in his electric blue flying scarf, through the haze of his shield and window. The lights from Tram's panel made his face look demonic; for an instant he was a demon, and his ship a bird of prey closing on Jason. . . .

Jason rejected the fantasy. Absurd. But it shook him.

Tram had been preying on his mind far too often during the last term. Jason was beginning to wonder if he were obsessed; his preoccupation with the other senior pilot troubled him. With an impatient shake of his head, Jason thrust thoughts of Tram aside. He could not afford introspection during grad exercises.

Some part of his mind, tightly locked away, was shouting a useless warning. Jason looked out his window, dodged a small planetoid, tracked onto the fox, and corrected his path. I won't freak, he thought. I won't twitch out. Not now. Too important. I won't lose to Tram.

There — behind a planetoid the size of

Collegium — his scanners caught a hint of energy leakage. The fox! Almost undetectable; it could be a glitch. He had to verify it before bursting around the planetoid; the turn and braking on the fox's side would be tricky, as the maze was heavy with garbage there. Jason slammed on his rets.

The computer did not respond. Somehow Jason had known it would not. He stared numbly while despair flowed through his muscles. His clawed hands lay heavy in his lap; he tried to lift them but they were rigid. Why bother? There was nothing he could do.

He knew what was about to happen and knew that all the corrections he would try would fail. His head lolled against his chest. Paralyzed. I am paralyzed. Terror reddened his vision.

With tremendous will, he lifted his head. That brief instant imprinted itself on his mind — his ship plummeting for the dark surface of the planetoid, back-up systems dead, alarms and his own voice screaming in his ears, and Tram shooting past him, with a vicious, triumphant smile that told Jason everything, the disbelief, outrage, terror, and the calm thought behind it all, I am about to die.

Andrea rested a hand on the slab, watching Jason's monitor. He was going to do it, he would beat the machine!

Then she leaned forward, surprised. Small anomalies had appeared, tangles and squirming knots in the loops of his fine motor coordination. They magnified, fed on themselves; his large motor coordination was going now, as well. Andrea had never seen anything like it.

Jason broke into a sweat and began to twist and writhe, his hands clenched on the sides of the table, his jaw working soundlessly. Then he twitched out. His readings went all over the screen.

"I'll get you!" His voice rose to a raw, high-pitched shriek of terror and rage that made Andrea's scalp crawl. *"Tram!"*

Instantly, guiltily, Andrea reached across him and shut down the machine. She snatched off the electrodes and lifted the dream specs off his head. He shot bolt upright and grabbed her arms, staring at her, pallid and wild-eyed. Then he forced his body to relax. Slowly, color came back into his narrow face, and he leaned back against the head rest with a smile that attempted bravado.

"How'd I do, Senior Colleague Pilot?"

Andrea looked at him for a moment through narrowed eyes, then gave him a grudging nod. She had to credit his self-control. It was not easy to have your wires stripped the way he had and come out with a smile, however shaky. Most cadets came out of the second-year fizz test trembling and complaining. And that was after two years of training. If his motor control had not broken down, he might have actually made it through that scenario. But she merely said, "Time for the psych tests, Candy."

She led him into another room, a small chamber with only a chair and a computer console. The arm rests on the chair glowed a soft lavender. The Eridanian stumbled on the plush carpeting as they entered the room, but when she reached out to assist him, he jerked his arm away with an angry glance.

"Look," she said. "There's nothing shameful about twitching out and needing assistance."

His face muscles lifted into a snarl. He was still thinking about his dragon, Andrea decided. Touchy as a cornered serpent.

"I don't need your sympathy, Senior Colleague Pilot. I'm doing fine."

"Have it your way," she said, disgusted. Then she became businesslike. Once he was seated she explained, "The computer will ask you a series of questions. All you're required to do is answer the questions and keep your palms on the chair armrests at all times."

He eyed the glowing armrests with an ironic smile. "Lie detectors, eh?"

"Just sit down and answer the questions," she snapped. How had he known?

Chapter 3

While the psych tests were being run, Andrea went to the cafeteria. She typed her order into the food dispenser, then sat down with a glass of Titan Delite. As she sipped the crimson juice, she twirled a lock of long, black hair. It was midafternoon, and the rows of white lucite tables were deserted. The lower classmembers would be getting out of class in a few minutes, at fourteen 'ten.

I'll get you. Tram. Andrea wondered what Jason had been dreaming of that could cause his control to degenerate so rapidly. Was it a phobia? Tram sounded like a nickname. Andrea tipped her glass down, then up, and absently watched the red protein fluid trickle down the sides of the glass.

It would be a shame if he had a serious phobia. She recalled the wild look in his cat-green eyes when she had removed the specs. *Tram.* He had not only been terrified, he had been outraged. The combination of phobia and anger could be deadly for a candy. In which case he would probably fail miserably on the psych test. She hoped not.

Then she scowled at herself. Less than two hours ago she had been hoping he would fail. But it would really be too bad to lose someone with his natural ability. The age factor was not really important, of itself; although, the younger a candidate was, the more flexible his or her response to training. But the Eridanian had shown a great deal of flexibility and self-control in the second-year fizz test, at least until his coordination blew out.

Andrea realized that her rash action might hamper Jason's responses to the third test, the gravity gauntlet test, if he passed the psych exam. That would really put my guilt into an open-ended do-loop, she thought.

Face it, Andy, she told herself. Those problems that showed up revealed some weird, strip-wired phobia. Either that, or you'll get back and find out that he has a classic case of the lone wolf syndrome, that he is categorically unable to work with others and will turn rogue at the first sign of trouble.

Young cadets began to flood into the cafeteria; Andrea, lost in her own thoughts, ignored them. They shouted and laughed, crowding around the dispenser behind her.

Suddenly, she heard someone shout in hostile tones, "Back of the line, goon."

A scuffle broke out. "You — terry trash — ! Back off."

Andrea spun around. Only the first few

cadets had seen that a senior pilot was sitting in the room; the few who noticed her now went pale and nudged their friends, who were gathering around the two antagonists at the dispenser. Andrea stood and shoved her way through the crowd of cadets. Everyone fell silent.

"It was just a joke, Colleague," someone ventured fearfully.

The two boys were crouched in the standard Collegiate fight stance. The older of the two had already bloodied the younger one's nose.

"Fall to," she snapped. They saw her, and their expressions disintegrated into dismay. They scrambled to attention. The crowd fell back.

"Senior Colleague," the older boy started, but faltered at the look she gave him. Then she spoke.

"Your names."

The younger boy licked the blood on his upper lip. "David Perensky, Colleague."

Completely red, the older boy stared at her. Then he tried to smile.

"Charles Aimes, Colleague. We weren't — "

"I don't recall asking for anything more than your name, cadet." Andrea gazed at him and the other boy until they began to sweat. There was painful silence among their classmates.

"Recite to me the Collegium Creed." She addressed the older boy, Aimes. He muttered the first few sentences.

"Louder," she snarled.

". . . to defend the neutrality of Collegium,"

he continued in an audible tone, "to treat all students, instructors, and school personnel with respect and in accordance with. . . ."

"That's enough." Andrea approached to within centimeters of his face. "Define goon," she said quietly.

The boy attempted another smile. He knew — everyone knew — that Andrea, the prov-valley this year, was a goon. One did not call the provisional class valedictorian any names, except, very politely, "Colleague." Aimes licked his lips; his gaze slid off her face. "Well, Colleague, I believe the word originated — "

"Define it in the context in which you used it."

He looked nervously over her shoulder at his silent classmates. "Everyone knows what a goon is, Colleague."

"Pretend I don't," she said sarcastically.

He said through tight lips, "It's a term for people who were not born on Earth. For people born in the Commonwealth."

"Would you consider it a term of respect, cadet?"

Suppressed titters rippled through the crowd.

"Colleague?" he stammered.

" 'Goon.' I want to know if you consider it a respectful term for a non-Terran."

"Well . . . I suppose it could be," he said. His face was absolutely deadpan.

"It appears you find this exchange humorous, cadet."

Color rose in his face. "No, Colleague, I — "

"Is 'goon' a term of respect?" she repeated with quiet intensity.

He lowered his gaze. Andrea read resentment as well as shame in his expression. "No, Colleague. It's usually used in a derogatory manner."

Andrea turned to face the younger cadet.

"I believe you used a similar expression."

The boy looked down. "I called him terry trash, Colleague. But...."

"I don't want to hear any excuses." Andrea turned her back and returned to her original position. "Collegium's charter is strict neutrality. You both know it. Racial, national, and religious differences have nothing to do with how good your crews are or whether you can trust your squadron members with your life. We cannot afford prejudice; your lives depend on whether you can work as a unit. Both of you," she leveled her finger at the boys, "have committed a serious infraction against Collegiate law."

She scanned the crowd. "You've all heard talk of impending war between the Earth Aggregate and the Trans-Martian Commonwealth. None of that should concern you. Political boundaries don't exist here. You swore to put that aside when you were dregs. When — if — you graduate, you might become involved in the war, if there is one. But while you are at Collegium, you do not bring your personal prejudices with you. We have no room for bigots and political fanatics."

A sea of wide eyes met her gaze. There was a shuffling of feet; they were ashamed. Good. She faced the two boys again. "Aimes."

The older boy stood forward. Fear flickered in his eyes.

"Colleague?"

"You insulted a fellow cadet and provoked him. You are expelled."

"What?" He gaped at her, then looked down as she ripped the chevron from his engineering tunic. His face went ashen. "You . . . you can't be serious . . . it isn't fair! Everybody does it!"

"You and you." Andrea picked two sophomores from the crowd. "Escort Aimes to Security and report to me in my quarters later."

The two cadets took Aimes by the arms and led him toward the door. "You're tracking with him because you're a goon, too," he screamed at her, shrilly. *"Goon!"*

His voice broke on the epithet and then faded behind the brilliant watercolors of the closing door. Andrea repressed a sigh and turned back to the younger boy. His lips quivered under her regard.

"You broke the Creed as well, Perensky."

His back straightened; he lowered his gaze and wiped the clotted blood from his nose. "Yes, Colleague."

"I realize you were provoked. But the pledge contains no excuses. Therefore, you are under level four probation for six months. If you are implicated in any further displays of this sort, even as a spectator, you will be instantly expelled. Do you scan me, cadet?"

He gaped at her, open-mouthed with stunned relief. "Yes, Colleague. It won't happen again."

"See that it doesn't. And the rest of you," she

turned to face the crowd, "log your names into the roster immediately. You are all under level one probation for three months, for treating this disturbance as if it were a spectator sport. There are," she did a quick count, "forty-seven cadets now present. If fewer than forty-seven names appear on my computer screen this evening, you and all other underclassmembers in this module will be put under level two probation, and I'll leave you to deal with the questions of your colleagues who weren't here today."

The crowd dispersed. Andrea sat down to finish her juice. She hated playing the Authority more than anything. But tension was growing, if she had ignored the incident there would have been injuries and bad feelings among the entire class. The curriculum alone provided enough stress to keep the cadets on the raw edge; a miniature civil war might have erupted.

Policy, she thought. Politics. She had just about had her fill of it. Collegium was supposed to be completely nonpolitical, but in practice — how could you force an entire population to forget its upbringing and firmly held beliefs?

Even the Collegiate Council's record was not pristine. An overabundance of "goon" applicants to Collegium during the past decade was starting to make Earth nervous, or so her friend Linc had told her. This meant there would be a sizeable number of top-flight pilots, engineers, scientists, and ship crews who had no particular loyalty to Earth. It had become standard policy for Earth-based governments and firms to use whatever leverage they could to keep goon cadets out of Collegium.

Since the 2030s Earth's governments and corporations had been pitted each against the other in a free-for-all power struggle over the fabulous wealth and resources of Mars, the asteriods, Jupiter, and Saturn. The trans-Martian communities were squeezed, pulled, and buffeted by political intrigues until the Amphitrite Action, back in 2092 and 2093, when a rich strike of cobalt and iridium had been discovered in the asteroids by reps of two different nations, almost simultaneously. The major players in the conflict for ownership abruptly discovered that the precious pawns they had so blithely expected to toady under them had minds of their own. And exquisitely sharp little teeth. And while they, the solar system colonists, were dependent on Earth and beholden to their parent companies, they had some clout, as well. In short, they could only be pushed so far. Within a year of the incident, the trans-Martian colonies had banded together and formed the Commonwealth.

Politics, Andrea thought again. She had always been a model student, one who followed the rules and enforced them. But she derived a certain amount of pleasure from contemplating successful acts of independence by others.

A pensive half-smile touched Andrea's lips. She curled her legs beneath her in her own small gesture of defiance and drained her glass.

Chapter 4

Back in the Pit, the candidates were seated in a row of chairs on one side of the antechamber. Andrea entered and approached Jan.

"Do you want to review the psych results before we continue?" Jan asked.

"Yes, we may as well save time." Andrea accompanied Jan into the back room and quickly reviewed the colored readouts for each candidate.

The Loonie's self-esteem was abysmally low, down in the red range, and she suffered from feelings of persecution and mild paranoia. She was out.

The older Terran was emotionally stable, having tested in the greens on most points, except for a substantial fear of failure, but he had already been eliminated as a mummy. His younger brother suffered from hero worship and had a tendency to avoid taking responsibility for his own actions. He might become a snitch or a drone; he was well in the red.

Andrea moved on through the readouts.

The Ethiopian girl was a wolfwoman! Way

in the red. Andrea was disappointed. The girl would have made a good pilot. But wolf tendencies were easily identified in the psych profile: self-important, highly individualistic, strongly self-motivated, combined with a powerful but suppressed need for approval, as well as a number of more subtle traits in various combinations.

The combination was deadly. Though aspects of the wolf profile were crucial in a good Collegium cadet, there was always a risk. To wit, would the candidate be able to channel this powerful independence toward constructive ends, or would he or she fly apart in a crisis and take his or her comrades down, too?

In the case of the Ethiopian girl, regrettably, Andrea had to choose the latter.

To her surprise, the Eridanian was high in the green range for most of his traits. He had no serious phobias, except for a moderate fear of suffocation. He was bordering red on wolf-man tendencies, but they were strongly compensated for by a fierce loyalty to friends and a great deal of personal integrity.

There were indications that he carried a grudge of some kind, a major one, which was rather uncharacteristic according to his psych readout. He was definitely an ace, though. Andrea saw nothing which should eliminate him. She sighed, unsure after all whether she was glad or dismayed, and turned to Jan.

"Looks like we've got ourselves a recruit."

She strode back into the antechamber and gestured for the four younger candidates to stand. Their faces registered nervous hope; the Eridanian sat with his legs crossed and his nylon duffel bag in his lap. The look he gave Andrea had a trace of sympathy in it that outraged her. He obviously knew what she was about to say to the others. How dare he be so sure that he was the only one chosen?

Andrea pressed her hands over her mouth and nose, eyeing the four young candidates. Then she dropped her arms. "Our tests indicate that, while all four of you have outstanding characteristics, you are unsuitable for training at Collegium. Your test results will be kept on file for five years. You may reapply to Collegium after two years and will be retested at that time. I am sorry," she said sympathetically, "and I wish you each the best of luck."

The techs led them into another room to collect their belongings and make departure arrangements.

Andrea turned to Jason. All evidence of his earlier empathy was gone; he leaned forward on an elbow, grinning at her.

"And you thought I'd fail," he said.

She lifted her eyebrows.

"You still might, Candy. There's one last test."

She took him to the gymnasium and handed him a leotard.

"Suit up, Candy. We're going to run you through the gravity gauntlet."

Jason eyed the leotard she handed him, then glanced back up at her with a sardonic smile that masked anxiety. The senior colleague pilot was as tall as he, slim-hipped, and had straight ebony hair that reached her waist. Her black eyes were glittering a challenge at him.

Jason estimated that she was roughly his age, seventeen. Her facial features, although not what he would classify as beautiful, were striking: a cool olive complexion, a wide nose, high, angular cheekbones, and a pointed chin. He knew from her features, if not from her name, that she was at least part Japanese, not that nationality meant a lot to the non-Terrans. And Jason had guessed from some of her mannerisms and her slightly tense, gravity-resistant posture that she was a Solarian colonist, rather than a Terran.

"What's the matter?" she asked him. "Finally getting nervous?"

Jason bit down an angry rejoinder. Of course he was nervous. The fact that he had lost control during the candy fizz test unnerved him. Under lower gravity his coordination and reflexes were fine, but at higher gees or under stress his responses to stimuli were unreliable. The therapists back on 40 Eridani II had tested him for a number of possible causes — injury-induced epilepsy, nerve damage — and then had shrugged and told him it was psychological. Their way of saying "I give up," Jason thought bitterly. Why didn't they just admit their inadequacy and be done with it?

Well, whatever its cause, he could not afford for it to happen twice during his harvest tests, or he'd be out for sure. And he could not use his

Collegiate training to remain in control, as he had during the fizz test, or this keen-eyed colleague would be suspicious.

Jason wished — not for the first time that day — that he had gotten a less perceptive cadet for an evaluator.

None of his doubts showed on his face. He merely grinned at her, replied to her taunt, "I can handle anything you throw at me, Colleague," and slipped the leotard on under his robe. Then he removed the gown, shrugged the leotard straps up onto his shoulders, and extended the cotton gown to her with two fingers.

With a curt nod, she took the robe and stepped out of the padded, spherical room. The door resolved behind her.

After a brief pause she appeared at the control room window above the door. She flicked on the transmitter. Her voice had a metallic echo to it.

"First we'll test your ability to move and keep your orientation in null grav."

Jason was abruptly weightless. He kicked gently off the floor and floated up to the window to face her, his arms folded and one leg crossed over the other. She frowned at him.

"This isn't a game, Candy. Notice the panel and chair on the far wall. You are piloting a ship which has suddenly lost acceleration." Her fingers tapped out a sequence on her control board. Then she looked up.

"The hull has been breached. Make your way through the debris back to the control panel and press the following buttons: first on the right, bottom row; second from the left, top row; and lastly the six buttons on the fourth row down, simultaneously. Remember, if you touch the debris it will deflect your trajectory, so avoid any collisions. Speed counts, so make it fast."

Jason turned. The room was filled with floating, holographic debris: twisted jags of machinery, a contour chair, and the body of a fellow "crewmember," either unconscious or dead. Nice touch, Jason thought. Really gruesome. He twisted back to look at the cadet.

"In a real situation I would be able to use the debris to correct my trajectory and propel myself."

"And risk tearing your pressure suit?" She smiled at him. "Don't be too sure of yourself; it isn't as easy as it looks. You learn the intricacies of null grav motion in your second year, if you last that long. Now stop arguing and do it."

He planted his feet on the window, directly before her face, and launched himself. It was almost too simple; he dove through the rotating jags of metal, curled himself around the "body" — allowing his leg to pass through it so as not to seem too expert — and grasped the back of the chair. It came away in his grasp; he spun slowly, out of control for a second, before righting himself with the handgrip beside the panel.

Dirty trick, he thought. I'd forgotten about that.

Jason glanced at the window and swiftly reoriented himself to "up" and "down," then pressed the buttons, although not too quickly; he was not supposed to be too good at this.

When he turned back, the debris was gone. Flickers of red and blue from the panel lighted the cadet's face as she studied his results.

"Well?" he said.

"You bumped into your comrade and were deflected, therefore you back-flopped against the wall next to the panel instead of reaching the chair. You ricocheted into the center of the room, tearing your pressure suit against a piece of debris. The cabin was depressurized before you got back to the panel and punched in the emergency shielding code." She looked up at him. "You're dead, Candy."

"If you're going to make elaborate projections, Colleague," he said angrily, "then give me the real thing. I would have found a way to compensate for that brush against the mummy."

She pierced him with a sudden, sharp look. "Where did you learn that expression?"

Jason winced inwardly, blaming his quick temper. "What expression? Oh, you mean the mummy." He laughed disdainfully. "Scan my stats, Colleague. My father's an exporter. I've been around Collegium graduates all my life. They've even given me a little preparatory training."

Her frown, which had been there since she had removed the dream specs from his head, cleared.

He would have to be careful to control his

tongue as well as his reflexes, Jason decided. It was hard to simulate a lack of knowledge, though. Collegiate lingo, or tongue-wag, came naturally to him now.

Well, the lie he had told her was a risky one, but at least it gave him a convenient excuse for knowing too much about Collegiate slang and traditions. As long as she didn't recheck the fictitious stats he had created and faxed to Sol, which listed his father as a mercantile dealer, he should be safe.

The tests proceeded. Jason discovered that his apprehensions had been groundless. The tests were simple. So simple, in fact, that he was able to feign clumsiness, hesitation, confusion . . . and still do what he knew to be extremely well, for a candy. His familiarity with the tests from his own days as duty officer helped. He began to remember in advance what sorts of surprises to expect and could allow the appropriate dismay and astonishment to come through, rather than automatic, trained responses.

Finally, Andrea disappeared from the control room. The door dissolved. Jason limped out of the room to meet her. The limp was not all contrivance, for the last tests, in six gees, had worn him out. His responses were still of graduate quality, but by Collegiate standards he had gotten a little out of shape.

Andrea was holding a brown, standard issue dreggie uniform folded across her arms. She held it out to him. Jason took it.

Two silver chevrons on the uniform caught

the light. Jason fingered them, his mind caught in a sudden, painful tumult. Pilot?

It's only because of my training, he thought. I'll never be what I was, I'll never get past the seizures. And it doesn't matter; I'm not here to be a pilot. All I require is a month at most.

He looked up at her.

"You're in, friend," she told him. "Welcome to Collegium."

Chapter 5

The Hammer sat at his desk in his spacious
private quarters under a yellow cone of light.
The rest of the room was in shadow. Andrea
paused at the doorway.

"Senior Colleague?"

He looked up. His face was smooth and oval,
and Andrea could feel his expressionless gray
eyes on her. He seemed annoyed by the inter-
ruption. Andrea shifted the fax board under her
arm.

"You requested a report on the harvest, sir."

"Yes, yes. Come in." He motioned her inside.

She approached his desk. The overhead light
shadowed his eyes, making them seem empty.
Andrea repressed a shiver.

"I recruited one candidate," she informed
him. "The rest were unsuitable."

"Let me see the test results."

She passed the board to him. As he leafed
through the glossy sheets, she glanced at the
faxes on his desk. Startled by their content, she
leaned closer, but his arm moved across them,
obscuring them. Then he handed her report back.

"Very good. Unusually high scores. He can be put in with the third trimester physics and astronomy freshmen. But you'd better bunk him with the seniors. We don't want him terrorizing the younger ones."

Jason won't be too happy about that, she thought dryly. They'll make his life miserable. "Yes, sir. I'll see to it."

After a moment, when she did not leave, he looked up at her again. "Is there something else?"

"There was a disturbance this afternoon in the cafeteria, a fight between two sophomores. I expelled the instigator and put the other under level four probation. I've logged my report into the roster."

He studied her briefly, then returned to his fax sheets. "Very good."

"Sir. . . ."

His voice had a titanium edge to it. "What is it, Colleague?"

"I'm concerned about the growing tension among the cadets, sir. This is the third fight we've had to break up this week."

He eyed her, pinching the bridge of his nose. "The solar system is on the brink of war, Colleague . . . Ito, isn't it?" Then his voice and expression softened. "These are tense times for all of us. But Collegium will ride out the storm. Tell your classmates to maintain strict control of the underclassmembers. I'd recommend an earlier curfew, if necessary. Use your own discretion." He flicked a hand at her. "Carry on, Colleague. That will be all."

She left the room with her mind in turmoil. The faxes on his desk had dealt with increased defensive capabilities. That was troubling enough, but one of the faxes had been different. Wrong, in some way she could not remember. She wished her glance had not been so quickly blocked. Well, she'd set her mind to it and see if she could bring it up from her memory.

It's probably nothing, she thought. Still. Still. . . .

Jason stood before the mirror in the little visitor's quarters where he had spent last night and looked himself over. Uggh. He picked distastefully at the sleeve of his brown freshman uniform. Me, valedictorian of the class of '87 — almost-valedictorian, he corrected himself, and the old pain stabbed at his stomach — wearing a dreggie uniform. If my old classmates could see me now. Then, with a mental shrug, he reached under his bunk and pulled out his duffel bag.

Collegium sure had changed in the last nineteen stay-years. The old school — his school, the massive toroid that trailed the new, modular version of Collegium like a steel skeleton caught in its wake — was empty and lifeless. The first sight of the old Collegium had wakened memories in his mind so vivid he could taste them. He had stared at the dead hulk, shocked, and a little sad. They had stripped great sections of its hull away for use in the new school.

The new Collegium was only eight years old.

It looked like a cluster of mushrooms, or an impossibly complex protein molecule, with clumps and chains of silver globes surrounded by a dozen asteroid mazes and dogged by the corpse of its predecessor. About all of this were the shield satellites, pricks of steel in neat pentagons. The shield network spread fans of energy that distorted vision and made the distant stars and asteroids flicker, as though Jason were gazing at them through an atmosphere.

Jason sat down on the bed and pulled the duffel bag onto his lap. He sensed Sssrei's impatience. Andrea had left him here, instructing him to pack up his things and change. She had promised to return for him in a little while; it had only been a couple of moments since she left, so he had time to make a quick check.

He yanked at the stubborn seam seal of his bag. The halves of the bag split, and he caught at the sphere of translucent silicone resin that tumbled out.

A welcome, flavored strongly with relief, greeted him at the touch, and slender glass filaments unfurled themselves from along the sides of the sphere. The double row of rubberlike spikes, which ran along the circumference of the Shenn's body, were retracted. Jason's companion was less than half a meter in diameter, and its texture was dry-oily, like cornstarch. Within the milky sphere of its body, warm eddies of liquid glowed. Its winglike photo-receptive membranes, which it used to absorb energy, were currently tucked away behind the fragile filaments. The creature looked more like some weird work of art than a sentient alien.

Jason gazed into the optical fibers of his companion with an apologetic grin.

"You took long," the alien's voice whispered into his mind, a touch reproachfully.

"Just a little longer, Sssrei," Jason replied. He set the silicone creature down on the pillow. "It's been a long day for you, too, I haven't forgotten. You're probably starving. I'll get you under a sunlamp as soon as I get settled in."

"If you could give me a few moments inside the convolver . . ." it suggested wistfully. Jason shook his head.

"I would if I could, friend. But I don't want anyone to know our little secret, yet. If I re-activate the convolver now, the energy leakage might be detected and traced. And I don't want to have to answer a lot of awkward questions about unusual modifications in my ship's drive. No, I want to appear to them as a garden variety Eridani yokel."

"I am uneasy with this . . . this . . ."

Jason suppressed a smile. "I believe 'vendetta' is the concept you're searching for, Sssrei."

". . . this diversion from the original plan," the silicone creature persisted doggedly. "If my people knew I was assisting you, they would hardly approve."

"But they don't." Jason gave the alien a wolfish grin. "Besides . . ." He began repacking the clothes that had fallen out of his bag. "I didn't get much argument from you the other day, when I proposed this little 'diversion,' as you so euphemistically call it." Again he sensed Sssrei's interest, and its skepticism, and again he wondered why Sssrei had finally agreed — albeit with some misgivings — to postpone its own desperate scheme in order to aid in his equally desperate plan.

It read his thoughts. "I have doubts about the practicality of this plan of yours," it said. "But I am interested. Between what you tell yourself you are doing, and the thoughts underneath, there is great conflict. And there is a bond between you and the Tram-human; among my people we call it enemy-bond. I want to see what happens."

"Do you?" Jason sealed his bag, suddenly annoyed. There was no bond between Tram and him. Jason had not seen him for almost three years, and for Tram it had been nineteen.

Tram was a monster. Jason wanted no bond with him. Only justice.

"Well, let me know what you decide about my motives, would you?"

Sssrei made no reply, merely drew back. Jason had the sense it was regarding him. "My friend," Sssrei replied after a moment, "it is not like motives that forge the chains of an enemy-bond, it is like *souls*."

With a sudden chill, Jason straightened and stared at Sssrei. A complex, disturbing tangle of emotions passed through him. As he gazed into the glowing tips of its filaments, he had the briefest glimpse into the subterranean depths of its alien mind. Vertigo clutched at his thoughts. . . .

He shuddered violently and, with a gasp, broke connection with Sssrei. Startled, the creature recoiled its filaments into its glistening body.

Jason drew a deep breath and cast a sharp look at the alien. Sometimes Sssrei was a little spooky. But Jason already had plenty to worry about, without stirring up doubts about Sssrei's motives, or a lot of Shenn mythology about telepathic enemy-bonds.

He drew his knees up and narrowed his eyes. He would have to find some excuse, some hobby that would allow him private access to the library computers. He had a lot of research to do.

There was a light footfall behind him; he spun around. Andrea Ito stood there.

"You have mighty good hearing, dreggie," she remarked. He frowned at her.

"Who taught you your manners?"

"You will address me respectfully, dreggie, either as Colleague or Colleague Ito, unless you want to go on report."

"I stand corrected. Who taught you manners, Colleague? Don't you believe in knocking before you enter? I might have been changing clothes."

She scowled, but made no rejoinder; obviously she had something on her mind. Instead, her glance wandered to Sssrei.

"What is that?"

Jason touched the murky ball of Sssrei's

body. "It's a silicone land creature native to 40 Eridani II."

She leaned closer, gazing at its smooth crystalline surface. A wondering look appeared on her face. "It's alive? It looks like a ball of quartz."

"Don't touch it," Jason said sharply as she reached toward it. She straightened, startled, then gave him a look of annoyance. "Don't touch it, *Colleague*," he amended. "Yes, it's alive. They exude a concentrated solution of ammonium hydroxide and cyclosiloxanes, when they're frightened. I wouldn't want you to burn your hands."

She looked at Sssrei. Jason got the feeling she would show more interest in it if it were not associated with him. "Pets are not allowed at Collegium, dreggie," she said. "Particularly not dangerous ones. You'll have to get rid of it."

Jason leaned back on his elbows. "Get rid of it? How? Colleague."

"I don't know. Throw it in the recycler, or something."

This wrung a telepathic cry of dismay from Sssrei; its propellant spikes slid out of their sheaths. Jason touched it soothingly. "Stay chill. I'm not going to let anyone throw you in a furnace," he thought. Aloud, he addressed Andrea, who was eyeing the alien with a reluctant fascination, "For your information, Colleague, this creature is one of an endangered species on 40 Eridani II. And it's not all that dangerous." Then inspiration struck. "And about the prohibition against pets — I believe an exception is made for animals with religious significance."

Andrea favored Jason with a raised eyebrow. He expected more of an argument from her, but she finally shrugged. She definitely had something big on her mind.

"Very well, you may keep your pet. As long as it makes no trouble. Come with me, I'll take you to your dorm."

He tucked Sssrei in among his clothes and resealed the seams of the bag, then slung it over his shoulder and followed Andrea into the hall.

Classes were letting out as they walked along. Jason noted that all of the younger cadets stepped back and eyed Andrea with awe. Even the older cadets were respectful toward her. She must be the provisional class valedictorian, Jason realized suddenly. He wondered briefly if she were as good a pilot as he had been.

Jason caught up with her.

"What's the destination, Colleague?"

She glanced at him sidelong. "You ask too many questions."

He grinned disarmingly at her. "I'm a curious sort," he replied, "Colleague."

She snorted. "That's for sure. Incidentally, if you persist in your exaggerated use of the honorific, I'll put you on report for insubordination."

Jason laughed incredulously. "On charges of calling you 'Colleague,' Colleague?"

"Precisely. And stop swaggering."

Swaggering? Jason thought. Andrea caught

his puzzled look and sighed with exasperation.

"You walk as if you own the whole corridor."

Jason choked down a laugh. "I would respectfully point out, Colleague, that you walk that way yourself."

"I'm a senior. You're a dreggie. If you carry yourself that way, someone's going to call you down for arrogance, and I'll have to expel you for fighting."

The muscles in Jason's cheeks twitched, but he kept a smile off his face. "That sounds like you want to keep me around for a while."

She froze him with a look. "Don't overstep yourself, dreg."

Then she stopped outside a door, unzipped her flight jacket, and pulled out some fax sheets. She handed them to him.

"Your schedule of classes, maps of the facility, and," she swept her arm toward the door, "your quarters. Good luck."

She turned on her heel and strode swiftly away. Jason watched her with an irrepressible smile.

"You know, Sssrei," he thought to the alien in his duffel bag, "I do believe she likes me."

Then her final words hit home, and Jason's smile faded slightly. Good luck? What an odd thing for her to say.

He stepped inside the dorm room, to find himself facing a room full of cadets his own age. She had bunked him, a dreg, with a class of seniors!

I'll get you for this, Ito, he thought, and, steeling himself, entered the room.

Chapter 6

Andrea hurried toward the rec module. It was eighteen 'fifty-two now; her classmates' rendezvous should be in full swing.

When she reached the rec center, her seven classmates were sitting on enormous gelatin pillows in the entertainment lounge, listening to music and eating pretzels. She sat down between Paul and her roommate Victoria and took a handful of the pretzels.

"Where'd you get these?" She popped one into her mouth. Although stale, they blasted the usual synthetic crackers right out of the sky.

Victoria lay back on her side with a languid smile. She was black, a Titan colonist with a deceptively calm veneer, a quick temper when challenged, and the highest scores in the class after Andrea. "Thomas bribed one of the cafeteria personnel with a promise to give him a run through one of the mazes during the prep runs next week."

Andrea cast an appraising look at Thomas, who waved at her from across the circle, his hands and mouth full of pretzels. Then she nodded.

"Commendable work, cadet."

"It was Weasel who found them," Thomas demurred.

"I should have known!"

Paul scowled at the nickname, then shrugged his shoulders with a modest smile at Andrea.

Paul asked her about the harvest, and what the Hammer was up to. He had been around even less than usual for the beginning of a term. Victoria leaned past Andrea to remark to Paul, "Who ever knows what the Hammer's up to? The mints never wag, and no one else ever sees him."

"He's planning something, though," Anya said. "Whenever he disappears into his quarters, you know he'll come out with some edict or some change in policy."

"I heard the launch techs say after supper that the Hammer has just prohibited incoming ships from docking," François remarked. "Both from the Solarian communities and from Earth. The only incoming ships will be drones with supplies from Ceres and Mars. Looks like he's expecting trouble. Big time."

"Either that," Victoria said, "or it's part of his plan to protect Collegium."

Andrea said reluctantly, "I don't know what he's planning, but it's something big. I only got a glimpse of the faxes on his desk, but I do know they had something to do with restructuring Collegium's defense systems. I suppose it's necessary, though."

Everyone exchanged looks.

Paul shook his head.

"Don't strip your wires, compadres. There won't be any fighting. Earth is sending a delegation of big mints to meet the Solarian junta." When everyone looked at him askance, he said, "Don't you trugs ever read the faxes? It's true. I read it at work a little while ago. The news just broke a couple of hours ago. They're meeting on Ceres with the Commonwealth leaders in a few weeks, to discuss a treaty."

Andrea sat back with a sigh. "Ultra-chill, if it's true."

"I swear it! On my honor."

Thomas scoffed. "You're slagging us, y la Vega. I read today's fax, and it didn't say anything about a peace conference."

Paul's jaw tightened; he glared at Thomas. "I'm not slagging anyone, compadre. It was right there on page one."

Thomas merely laughed disparagingly. Andrea stared in horror. The tension had even infected her own classmates.

"That's enough," she said sharply. "Chill it, both of you."

Paul, who had risen to a half-crouch and clenched his fists, looked at her and then shrugged. "Whatever you say, carita. But I didn't lie."

Thomas started to speak, but Andrea shot him a look, and he remained silent.

Victoria exchanged glances with Andrea. "Turn up the music," she said. The student by the panel adjusted the volume, and talk turned to their upcoming finals. But the congenial atmosphere had been destroyed and everyone's mood had soured. Andrea was almost relieved when the transmitter on her chronometer buzzed, and her presence was requested in the med center.

"Duty calls," she said and stood.

Victoria followed her into the hall. "Andrea, wait a second." She caught up with Andrea and took her arm. "There's something you're not telling the rest of us, isn't there? You've got that no-wag look on your face. What did Hammer say today?"

Andrea sighed. She did not want to start any rumors. "I don't think I should tell anyone, Victoria. I may be tracking onto ghosts."

Victoria looked at her for a long moment. Her mouth tightened and her eyebrows went up. "Well, it's up to you." She turned to go back inside the rec center.

"Victoria," Andrea started. Her classmate turned. "I'm not turning rogue. It's just that, well, something's going on, but all I have right now is an intuition. I don't want to start a lot of talk until I know more."

Victoria regarded her, then nodded. "Okay. But if you need any help, Colleague, let me know."

Andrea gave her arm a grateful squeeze and then hurried toward the med center. She had been thinking furiously since she had left the Hammer's office.

She had not really had a chance to read the faxes on his desk. But what had disturbed her about that one fax that his arm had blocked was dawning on her. It did not seem possible, but she could no longer deny it, even to herself. One of the Hammer's faxes had dealt not with defense, but with *offense*. He was planning some sort of offensive strike.

It could not be true. Collegium was strictly neutral. She must have misread the fax. The mind could play tricks when it did not have enough information. And besides, sometimes one had to plan an offense in order to defend oneself.

That would explain it. It was the only explanation that made any sense.

The worry that had haunted her since her report to the Hammer faded, and she even laughed at herself for her earlier doubts. She had a simple case of the pregraduation twitches.

Chapter 7

The med center was on the far side of Collegium, about two miles away through meandering passages. Andrea decided to take a gravity shuttle.

The shuttle was a glass and metal sphere with a cushioned couch and an input console. Andrea climbed into the couch, lay down and fastened the webbing across herself, and then punched in her destination. The door slid closed, and the shuttle's gravity field energized. Then it slid from its nook and accelerated.

The shuttle slowed as it neared one of the outermost modules. It settled into a nook, and the gravity field deactivated. Andrea unhooked her webbing and climbed out. She was a little dizzy. Riding the grav-shuttles was wilder than any amusement ride she had ever ridden in any submarine city of Europa.

The walk from the shuttle to the emergency room was a short one. Antiseptics stung Andrea's nostrils as she debarked the shuttle. She turned down a branch corridor. A tall, lanky man leaned against the wall outside the med center, his arms folded. He wore an expression of tired patience.

Andrea's eyes went wide; she gasped. Then a broad smile came onto her face.

"Linc!"

He turned and registered surprise as she approached him. "Andy?" he asked tentatively, squinting at her. Then he broke into a pleased, face-wrinkling smile and hugged her.

"I was planning on looking you up," he told Andrea, releasing her. He looked at her closely. "My God, how you've grown."

She scrutinized him; he looked as fit as ever. He had headed an expedition to Proxima Centauri while she was still in primary school and had spent the last eight years in dial-time, so of course he had not changed. It had only been a couple months at most, to him.

Dave Turin was a Europan, and a close friend of her parents. His nickname, Linc, was their private joke. At the age of eight, when she was studying Old American History in primary school, Andrea had decided that Dave, with his chiseled features and stooped stance, looked like Abraham Lincoln. The name had stuck.

"What are you doing on Collegium?" she demanded. "How long have you been here? And how long will you stay?"

He laughed. "Chill yourself, child, I'll be here a while yet. Standard check-up, I've been out-system for a few weeks and they want to make sure I'm healthy."

"A few weeks! It's been years." Andrea

took his hand. "How long have you been back? Have you been to Europa yet?"

He gave her an intense look, but merely nodded. "I have a faxcomm for you from your family. I'll give it to you later."

"Well." Andrea scowled. "Why are the physicians keeping you waiting out here in the hall?"

He grinned wryly. "Seems there was a commotion in the dorm. One of the underclassmembers injured a couple of seniors." He jerked his head toward the open door. "They're in there now."

Andrea winced. "I forgot. Excuse me, Linc. I'll be back in a few minutes."

The Eridanian dreggie, Jason, was sitting in the waiting room between two burly, stone-faced seniors. He threw a defiant look at Andrea. His pet was in his lap, and his face was covered with cuts and bruises. Andrea paused and frowned at Jason. She should have guessed he was at the center of this.

"I'll deal with you later," she told him.

She strode into the treatment room. Two seniors were lying on examining tables. The physician was bent over one of them. The other looked away when she glanced at him. His arm was submersed in a metal basin. Both seniors had taken quite a beating — presumably at Jason's hands; one of them had a split lip and a broken rib, and the other had two black eyes. That dreg might be a royal pain, Andrea thought, but he sure knew how to fight.

Andrea got the story from the physician,

after she had treated the two seniors. The woman pulled off her gown and took Andrea into her office. They sat down on the gel couches.

"None of the boys will talk about it," she said, sliding her spectacles onto her nose, "but from what I can gather, the two seniors somehow came in contact with the Eridani creature, and it sprayed them with ammonium hydroxide. The freshman wouldn't let me take the creature, but he did tell me how to treat the burns."

Andrea clenched her jaw. *Not dangerous.* She'd bought into it; she was as responsible for this as anyone.

"Will they be all right?"

"Oh, they're fine," the woman replied. "The solution was neutralized quickly enough to prevent any damage to them."

Well, he's out, Andrea thought of the Eridanian. The thought did not make her happy. The physician read Andrea's expression and leaned back, removing her glasses.

"I have nothing to do with discipline, Colleague," she said, "but obviously the two seniors are just as responsible for what happened as the freshman. I get to treat all the injuries the seniors inflict on the underclassmembers, so I know what goes on when no one's around to report these things.

"And the library contains a little information about these creatures: they are completely inoffensive unless gravely threatened. I suspect the seniors were tormenting the creature, and it retaliated."

Andrea sighed. "Well. He did tell me the

creature wasn't dangerous, unless it was afraid." She stood. "Well, thanks for the information — and the advice."

As she returned to the treatment room, one of the seniors was saying, ". . . you for this, dreg!"

"I warned you," Jason replied simply, as Andrea entered. Then all five of the students looked up at her. "You two." She gestured at the seniors guarding Jason. "You're dismissed. Return to your quarters."

Simon, one of the two who had been injured, stood.

"I hope you're going to take appropriate measures, Colleague," he told Andrea.

"You're right, I am," she replied shortly. "You are both on report for harassing a freshman."

Both seniors cried outrage, but she cut them off. "Get out of here. And consider yourselves fortunate that I didn't expel you outright."

Simon came toward her threateningly; she stood her ground and looked him squarely in the eye. "One more step, Colleague, and your career is finished."

He pointed a finger at her. "You'll pay for this, Ito. Mark my words."

She flicked a contemptuous hand at him. "Slag off, Simon. You knew the rules, and you violated them."

His friend took his arm. "Come on, let's get out of here."

They left. Jason was looking at Andrea, and there was surprised admiration in his gaze.

Neither of them said anything for a moment.

"Thanks," he said finally.

"Don't thank me. You obviously can't control your pet. It has to go. Now."

"It has the right to defend itself. They were using it for a volleyball — they could have killed it."

"Doesn't matter. It's still got to go."

A look of desperation came onto his face; he grabbed her hands. "Andrea, please. There's no place I could send it. You — you don't know how important it is." He swallowed. "Please."

Andrea pulled her hands free in consternation. She had not expected a plea. Defiance, anger, yes. But not this. She studied him for a long moment, then eyed the creature. Finally, she tossed her hands up.

"Fine. Keep it. Until the next outbound ship docks. Then you send it back to 40 Eridani II."

His face clouded with anger. "And who'll make sure it doesn't die en route? They need special care; you can't just put Sssrei in a box and put postage stamps on it. . . ."

"You can send along a list of instructions. Your family is wealthy enough to afford the cost, I'm sure."

Jason locked gazes with her. Then he stood. He bit down on whatever he had been about to say and tucked the creature under his arm.

"Thanks for being so understanding."

Dave walked into the room just as Jason stormed out. Dave looked after the Eridanian. He appeared startled, then thoughtful.

"What was that all about?" he asked her.

Andrea sat down in the chair. "I hate being duty officer. Why couldn't this have happened on someone else's day?" At Dave's querying look she added, "I had to make him get rid of his pet, and I feel like a rat. He told me earlier that the creature had religious significance to him, and I was pretty sure he was lying. But apparently it does — he sure got upset when I told him he'd have to send it back to Eridani."

Dave burst into laughter. "Religious significance? Child, you've been had. Those creatures have about as much significance to the colonists as a dirty kleenex. They're everywhere on 40 Eridani II, or were, for a while."

Andrea stared at him, aghast. "What?"

Dave nodded. "I have all my grandfather's old correspondence. According to his letters those creatures were real pests when the colonists first arrived. They kept getting into the machinery and people's houses and the like, giving people chemical burns and so on. After the colonists killed a few of them the rest disappeared. I'm real surprised to see a colonist with one for a pet."

Andrea went hot. "That slime!"

Dave seemed amused. "Well, you have to give him points for originality." Then the same thoughtful look he had had a couple moments earlier came onto his face. "I don't know why, but he really looks familiar to me."

Andrea's thoughts were running along other lines. That dreggie was up to something. And Andrea Ito did not like to be lied to.

Chapter 8

"I am truly sorry, Jason."

Jason had brought Sssrei to the cafeteria, in a module near the science college's dorms. He could not make himself go back to the dorm just yet.

The alien was emanating dismay and guilt. "I am sorry."

Jason cast Sssrei a brief look. "Not your fault, friend. I should never have involved you in this. It was my fault. If they had dropped you . . ."

"Jason." Sssrei's optic fibers touched his cheek. "We are friends. You saved my life, back on Shenndri. Now I owe you two lives."

Jason laughed, a harsh bark. "You owe me nothing, Sssrei. I've brought you into a hostile place, where no one knows you're sentient — or would care if they did know. I coerced you into being a party to this private vendetta of mine. It'll be harder to pull off by myself — but no, Ito is right. I'll send you back on the next ship."

"I refuse." The alien's mind-voice was steel. Jason glanced at it in astonishment. It went on more gently, "Jason-human, you say you've coerced me. You are mistaken. When you saved me from death in the caverns of glass and our minds joined, I saw far more of your life than you did of mine. I know the reasons for what you're doing. If I had wanted to stop you I could have. I am here not only to petition your race, but to observe. I will not be sent away. I will remain with you."

Jason eyed the alien, suddenly uncomfortable. Just how much do I really know about them? he thought. The glimpses he had had of Sssrei's mind had terrified him — its body was fragile, but its mind was frighteningly powerful.

After their first merging, Sssrei had kept vast areas of thought and emotion hidden behind impenetrable walls. Jason had assumed Sssrei had merely been protecting him . . . but what if its purpose were more sinister?

Jason was only marginally telepathic, and occasionally Sssrei had to strain to maintain the contact between them. What if he were wrong about the Shenn? What would Sssrei do? Destroy his mind? Jason was convinced Sssrei could, if it wanted to.

No. During their mind merge, Jason had not understood everything he had seen and felt in Sssrei's mind; he had not been brought up as a functioning telepath, as Sssrei had. But he had seen enough to know that Sssrei — and its people — had a code of ethics; they respected other life, however different. They would defend themselves from humans if necessary, but they would not do harm, if there were another way.

But its people were desperate — on the verge of extinction. Who could say what they would do, really?

Jason shrugged, annoyed with himself. So what? I could kill Sssrei, he thought, simply by holding it two meters above the floor and dropping it. And it could probably wipe my mind out and make me a gibbering idiot with a simple thought. So what have we got if we don't have trust?

"All right, Sssrei," he said softly. "You win. I'll do what I can. If we have to, we'll hide you. And hope Ito doesn't catch on."

Andrea found Jason in the cafeteria. He sat alone at a table, picking a styrofoam cup to bits. Andrea came up to his table and saw the little alien on the chair next to him. Her anger ebbed out of her at the look on Jason's face. He looked as if someone had just told him his best friend had died.

"May I join you?" she asked. Jason seemed startled to see her. Then he shrugged.

"Sure."

Andrea leaned forward on the table. "Look, Stiletto. I found out your pet is no religious icon. I came here to chew you out for lying to me. I haven't put you on report, but what am I supposed to do? You come here with an attitude that'd get anyone dumped, your animal burned two students, and I find out your story about this alien being some sort of religious symbol is all garbage. Tell me. If you were in my position, what would you do? I'm curious."

Jason gave her a look filled with weariness. "Do whatever seems best, Colleague. I don't care."

Andrea frowned at him for a moment. She finally shrugged. "Slag it; I'm off duty in twenty minutes, anyhow."

She threw an arm over the back of her chair. "So. You want to talk about what's eating you?"

"No." His tone was brusque, and he would not meet her gaze.

"Look, Stiletto — I'm trying my best to like you, but you're sure not making it easy." She stood. "So you aren't willing to make friends here. Fine. You go right ahead playing mysterious stranger. But I can tell you right now, if you're not willing to accept friendly gestures from others, your four years here are going to be mighty cold and lonely ones."

His gaze met hers and locked. "I thought I wouldn't be lasting six weeks," he said, but there was no acid in his tone, and his voice was low. Then he dropped his gaze to the shreds of the cup and continued tearing them.

"You are truly hopeless." With a sigh of exasperation, Andrea turned and left.

The dorm was dark when she got back, except for the light from a desk lamp. Victoria was still awake, studying. Anya and Nöel were in bed. Victoria looked up and saw her expression.

"Anything serious?"

Andrea waved a hand. "Nah."

"What happened?"

She did not feel like talking about it and shook her head at Victoria's curious gaze. "Just a dreg who thinks he doesn't need any friends."

Victoria gazed sharply at Andrea, her eyebrows arched.

"What?" Andrea asked, shortly. Her roommate's lips twisted into a smile, but she only pointed at Andrea's bed.

"Commander Turin came by earlier and left that."

A faxcan lay on her bed, with a note attached.

Andy — Stopped by to deliver this and you weren't here.

Lots going on. We'll talk later. — Linc

Andrea frowned at the note. *Lots going on.* Linc had always been such a slagging tease. He had obviously heard news about the political winds, or perhaps something had happened during the Proxima Centauri expedition, and he couldn't resist being mysterious about it.

She broke the can's seal and pulled out the faxsheet. It was a letter from her mother, a chatty note that said little. But sealed onto the sheet, beneath the signature, was a whisperchip. As Andrea fingered it, a sudden twinge of anxiety fluttered in her stomach. *In case we*

need to contact you privately . . . the password
will be HALLOWEEN.

She hesitated for a moment over whether to put off reading it till morning. Final simulations began tomorrow, and it had been a long, exhausting day. And curfew started in seven minutes. But technically she was still duty officer, so curfew did not apply to her.

"I'll be back in a minute, Vic," she said. She tucked the fax into her pocket and hurried to the library.

She logged onto the computer and requested an open-front run. The console's activity light came on and, after several questions about the type of program and the language protocol, it finally printed

INPUT DATA CHIP.

Andrea lay the chip in the fingernail-sized depression just above the keyboard. A thread of red light appeared from beneath the crystal chip and moved across its surface. The screen cleared, and then displayed

S-s-s-h-h!
WHISPER-CHIP : THE ULTIMATE IN SECURED
COMMUNICATIONS!
BROUGHT TO YOU BY FAXCOMM, INC.
FAXDROP N8201-C
SERENDIPITY STATION,
L-5(6),
EARTH 0107753.

ENTER PASSWORD —

Andrea typed in HALLOWEEN, hit the RETURN key and sat back. The screen cleared again.

8/18/06
Andrea,

I hope the whisper-chip didn't alarm you.
Your father and I considered putting some
of this in the fax, but we decided that
under the circumstances a little caution
might be in order.

I'm sure you've read the newsfaxes; war
with the Earth Aggregate seems immi-
nent. They are threatening to cut off our
grain and machinery imports. The E.A. is
attempting to strike at the Commonwealth
piecemeal, colony by colony, but so far
we're hanging together. People are getting
scared, though — Shiro projects three
weeks, maybe a month, before things blow.

Dave has just returned from Proxima
Centauri. A classified project has been
under way for twelve years, sponsored by
the E.A., to colonize Proxima Centauri V.
If war breaks out, Commonwealth citizens
will be restricted. We've applied for resi-
dency there for us and the boys, and have
paid for expedited processing. By the time
you receive this, all the papers should have
been processed. We've applied for you as
well.

Whether you come or not is your decision,
Andrea. If you decide to come with us, you
must reach Europa by the tenth of Sep-

tember. Dave has agreed to transport you here. If you decide to stay behind we'll understand. But do think it over, dear — if a war starts, the entire solar system might be wiped out. Neither side will last long without the other.

We love you very, very much.

Mom

Andrea read the message several times, and then cleared the screen. Trick or treat, she thought. There was a dull ache in her stomach.

Today was August 29th. Since Collegium and Jupiter were within two degrees of conjunction, travel time would be about four days. So she still had a week to make up her mind.

Mechanically, she erased the message. She hunched her shoulders and folded her legs under her. Leave Collegium, two weeks before graduation? After four years, after working so hard and for so long? With a sigh, she dug her fingers into her hair.

Chapter 9

Jason sat on a catwalk, kicking his legs impatiently over the side. Twenty meters below, within the transparent pipes of the fusion reactor's heat exchangers, fluid glowed a dazzling orange and gold. Jason could feel the heat and smell the sweet, oily fumes of the fluid that had escaped containment and puddled on the floor around the exchangers.

The fluid roared like an outraged beast as it swirled and coalesced within the pipes. Jason had to appreciate the spectacle despite his impatience.: Sssrei, a black speck next to one of the exchangers, was enjoying a feast.

Hurry up, Sssrei, he thought, but did not transmit it. He had signed up to use a library carrel in ten minutes, and if he didn't show up on time he'd lose the time slot. But the little alien needed light to survive, and Jason had been so busy over the last week that Sssrei had had to go without.

Freshmen did not ordinarily get access to private carrels. But Jason had made a bet with his Field Theory instructor that he would make a 100% on the term's first test. Paul Omungo was a sarcastic, scruffy-bearded black man with an enormous belly, who had been exiled from Kenya many years before as a political radical. He took his frustrations out on the students by insulting and humiliating them in class. However, he was an adequate teacher, all things considered, and believed in rewarding success. Jason and he had been exchanging banter since the first day of class — and he had laughed yesterday when Jason had made his proposal.

"No one makes a hundred on my tests, dreg."

Jason, remembering now, touched the plastic access card he'd won in his pocket, and smiled. And, one more time, willed Sssrei to hurry.

Finally in tones of pleased satiation, Sssrei sent him a message to come down. Jason raced down the steps into the blast of heat. He scooped Sssrei up and darted toward the door, his boots making a clamor on the metal steps. Three minutes. He'd just make it.

Several students gave him suspicious glances as he sat down and keyed into the computer, but no one bothered him. After his fight the first night people had pretty much left him alone. Jason set Sssrei down on the table and lay a magneto-stylus beside the keyboard.

He had no back doors into Tram's personal files; they would be enshrouded within a no-man's-land of passwords and trapdoors. Jason did not think he would need them, in any case. He knew how to get into Collegium's administrative and financial files, from his days as a senior colleague. And he also knew how Tram's mind worked. He had had firsthand experience of that.

Jason had given the matter a good deal of thought. He had analyzed Tram with the intense, dogged logic he had used to become valedictorian of his class. Trammerden, Jon: motive, method, opportunity.

Trammerden was cunning and intelligent, but he was not subtle. He always took the shortest line between two points, so whatever he was planning would be streamlined and simple. He would want political power, and he would seek the simplest, quickest method of obtaining it. Jason had put all of this together during the year and a half he had spent in physical therapy, back on 40 Eridani II. What had been missing was opportunity.

But with the explosion of news that followed Joan Tolyer's development of a unified field theory, and the subsequent taming of gravitational waves as a means of communication, a few months ago the 40 Eridani star system had begun to be inundated with news of current events beamed from Sol at thirty thousand times the snail's crawl of light.

Jason had caught up on the faxes recounting the several years of political tensions. And he had known, somehow, Tram would make an opportunity of the uneasy political situation. Deceit and subversion were his specialty. And as Senior Administrator of a highly acclaimed, politically neutral flight academy isolated from the war's fallout in a mineral-poor stretch of planetoids, a fine opportunity he would make of it, too.

Jason knew what Tram was up to. He knew with a conviction so great it occasionally frightened him. All he needed was proof.

He got to work.

Two hours later Jason left the terminal with Sssrei under one arm, a manila envelope filled with microfaxes under the other, and a grim smile on his face. *I had you figured right, Tram. I've got you.*

He hid the microfaxes and notepad in the generator module. Jason figured the evidence would be safer there than anywhere else; it was off-limits and too uncomfortably warm for anyone — anyone but Jason — to bother breaking the security code to make it his secluded spot. Then he took Sssrei back to the dorm.

A couple of seniors were there, but they ignored him. He sensed Sssrei on the fringes of his mind as he tucked it carefully in the footlocker at the base of his bunk, but Sssrei did not respond to his querying thought, and his own mind was too occupied for him to pay much attention to Sssrei's silence. Jason left the footlocker open in case Sssrei wanted to look around over its edge; the little alien should be safe enough at the moment.

His search had given him all the verification he needed. Trammerden had spent the last six years funneling massive funds into fortification of the new school's defense systems — to the point where Collegium was probably the best-defended installation in the entire solar system. Jason had records of contracts with all the major military manufacturing corporations for hardware, software, state-of-the-art weaponry, computers, and craft. Even in a war, neutral Collegium would not need such a vast array of defensive and offensive weapons systems. It was all the proof Jason needed.

Tomorrow he would fax copies to the heads of the Earth Aggregate and the Trans-Martian Commonwealth. Jason lay on his back and propped his head on his arms. A smile spread across his face. I have you, Tram, he thought. I have you. I wish I could see your face when the questions start coming.

"Jason?"

He looked between his stockinged feet at the footlocker. Sssrei had extended its optic filaments over the edge of the bed.

"I do not know humans well," it said. "But among my people, proposals submitted by the young are largely disregarded. I have observed a similar tendency among your people."

Apprehension clenched Jason's gut. He propped himself on his elbows and regarded the alien. "What are you trying to say, Sssrei?"

It was silent a moment. "Jason, it took me a long time to persuade my people to allow me to try and contact your race one last time. My proposal was sound, my logic infallible, and still they resisted. Because I am young.

"I have overheard some of your thoughts. It occurs to me that this Trammerden may very well have some contingency plan in place in case he is asked about these weapons. If you challenge him now, you risk not succeeding in your vendetta at all. You might merely alert him to your presence and lose your advantage."

Jason rested his chin on his hands. After a moment, he said, "You're right. Tram was never one to leave loose ends lying around. I need something definite — something he can't refute or explain away."

He slammed his fist into the bed. "But how? There's no way I can access his files; he had the edge on me, when it came to programming, even back when we were seniors. And he's bought all kinds of computer security software . . . there's no way I can break into his files. How can I get proof positive?"

"I don't know, Jason." There was concern and sympathy in Sssrei's thoughts. "Perhaps you'll think of something."

"Right." Jason shoved himself off the bed. "Sure. Listen, I'm going to go work out. I'll be back in a while."

He locked Sssrei in the footlocker, snatched his sweats off the hook at the head of his bed, and checked the log display on the wall. No one had signed up to use the gravity gym; all the seniors were out on exercises. He logged in for an hour, and headed for the gym.

September fifth. The day had come. How many hours did she have before it was too late to decide? Six?

Andrea's hand paused over her control panel. Four wolves, simulated enemy ships, showed up on her screen, angling in at two hundred sixty-two degrees theta, seven degrees phi, their screens up and scanning fight-ready. This was no time to brood.

Swiftly, she programmed evasive maneuvers into her computer. Then she cut back her speed just a little. As seconds passed, the wolves gradually began to gain on her. Hold course, Andy, hold . . . Beads of sweat formed on her face. If she veered too soon the wolves would be right on her tail, but if she waited too long she would be wiped across space by their lasers.

They were almost in range. A weak, premature shot sizzled past above the cockpit window. She held her course.

Her holo-tracker lit up. They were in range. She could only see empty space. Open run; no place to hide. If she could wait a couple of seconds more. . . .

Several bursts of blinding, scarlet light pulsed around her ship in rapid sequence. Her craft trembled at their passage. They were closing; the next shot would finish her. It was time.

She fueled the engines and went into a sickeningly sudden arc — she was slammed against her seat. She struggled for breath. Count to ten, Andy. You can stand it. Five gees, six . . . eight-point-one. Her chest contracted and her face muscles were remolded like clay. Her face a mask of sheer will, Andrea forced her arm up to shut off the acceleration. The pressure relented; Andrea caught her breath, swiftly reevaluated her new position, and programmed several probable trajectories into the computer.

She had circled around and was coming up behind them. Her tracker reactivated as she approached. They were trying to turn and meet her fire, but they were too late. They crossed the range of her guns as they scattered. She took out the first two without even needing a course correction and then tracked onto and blew away the third. Her craft shot through debris and glowing vapor.

She sat back with a sigh and switched off her trackers. I have to decide what I'm going to do. No more time. Should I go?

Abruptly the computer screamed a warning — wolf on her tail, close range, at one hundred eighty-one theta, zero phi! Andrea slammed her scanner back on. There had been four wolves. *Four.* How could she have been such a wipe?

The two seconds it took to evade a close-range attack were too many. Her ship began a wild climb; a red halo engulfed the craft and the last thing she heard was the escape of air and the concussion shattering her ears as her ship exploded and turned molten around her.

Andrea swept off her simulation specs, threw them on the floor, and kicked them across the room. A tech was disengaging the simulator. He avoided her gaze. She did not check her score.

She went out into the corridor, shoved her fists into her pockets, and leaned against the wall. In a few minutes, Victoria and Paul strolled out, laughing and talking.

". . . I noticed when they were tracking on me that the fourth one was back far enough to shadow me, so I programmed in an infinity roll," Victoria was saying. "I didn't think I'd be able to recover before I blacked out. But it worked — I threw the wolf into a gee-hole trying to keep up. By the time I wiped the others he was out of control and floundering in front of my guns."

Paul grimaced. "I just tried the old stand-by, a high-gee belly roll. Nearly missed the fourth one; he turned tail while I was frying his compadres."

Victoria spotted Andrea, and slapped her on the shoulder. "How'd you finish them, valley?"

Andrea gave Victoria a smouldering look. "I got wiped," she said flatly. Victoria's dark eyes went wide. She and Paul exchanged a look.

"So I made a mistake," Andrea said brusquely. Paul and Victoria glanced at each other again; their expressions only made her angrier.

After an awkward silence, Paul said, "Everyone gets wiped, Andy. It's no big deal."

She spun on him. "Don't tell me it's not a big deal, Weasel. If that had been real I'd be dead."

Paul's expression went stony. After a moment, she said, "Sorry. I'm angry with myself. I shouldn't have taken it out on you."

Paul shrugged without meeting her gaze. Andrea winced. Dumb, Ito, she thought. Real dumb. Mere days before finals is not a good time to dump on your friends. She and Victoria exchanged a look; they started walking.

Then Paul drew a breath and gave her a side-long look. He touched a finger to her jaw. "Next time you get your screens wiped, carita, take it out on the sim tech or somebody. I got enough troubles."

Andrea gave him an apologetic smile. "Whatever you say, Weasel."

"And stop calling me Weasel."

Victoria echoed his rejoinder perfectly, in both words and intonation. The three of them looked at each other, burst into laughter, and embraced swiftly.

"Food," Victoria said in a baritone. "Now."

She sprinted down the hall, and Paul and Andrea ran to catch up, laughing. Eventually they slowed to a panting, giggling walk.

They passed the gym and saw that the occupied light was on.

"Wonder who's working out?" Victoria remarked. "I thought the whole upper class was scheduled for simulations."

They went inside the control room. Inside the gymnasium, the Eridanian dreg was working out. Andrea leaned on the panel and scrutinized him while her friends watched over her shoulder.

He had pitted himself against the sparring robot. Right now the Eridanian was bent over, breathing heavily. His hair hung lank and wet about his face. Tremors of exhaustion shook his muscles. The robot stood just outside his range, a squat, beige parody of a human with a plasteen dome for a head and a cam-I camera mounted where its nose should be. Someone, years before, had painted huge blue eyes and a grotesque red grin on its face.

Victoria touched Andrea's arm and pointed at the control board. Paul's glance followed Victoria's gesture.

"Sparring in two-point-eight gees!" Paul exclaimed, surprised. "Now that's a dreg with machismo."

"Either that, or he likes pain."

"You recruited him, didn't you?" Victoria asked Andrea. She nodded thoughtfully, watching him through narrowed eyes.

"Let's get something to eat, compadres." Paul started out the door. Victoria glanced at Andrea, who shook her head.

"I want to hang around and watch him for a while," she said.

Once Victoria and Paul had left, Andrea sat down in the contour chair. After a couple of minutes Jason straightened and tapped the robot on its dome to reactivate it. Its sensory camera swiveled and focused on him, then it approached him. They circled each other warily.

He was using Collegium sparring techniques. His friends back on 40 Eridani II sure had done a thorough job of training him, Andrea thought. The dreg and the robot exchanged swift, jarring blows; there was an abrupt, vicious tangle. Jason locked the robot in a vise, trying to throw it to the floor.

The computer before her tallied damage. He was using killing force against the automaton. Andrea raised her eyebrows; this was getting interesting.

The robot threw itself backward onto him. Andrea grimaced — those things were heavy enough at normal gees. He'd be lucky to escape without several broken ribs.

The robot rose and backed up while Jason staggered to his feet. He lowered his head like an enraged bull. The look on his face was terrifying. He lashed out with a foot, a fist; the robot dodged and they spun to face each other again. Then Jason closed with the sparring robot again and pounded its chest pads with his fists, making the robot's damage readings soar.

He was slowing, though. The automaton snapped a blow across his face that made drops of blood fly; he went spinning and slammed against the padded wall, slumping to the floor. Jason forced himself halfway to his feet, but the robot was already on him; grinning, it grabbed his hair and with mechanical regularity began to drive its blunt-ended arm into his face and chest. Andrea reached forward to shut the automaton down. This had gone on long enough.

As she shut the sparring machine off, Jason tore free of its grasp with a grunt and scrambled away. He collapsed on the floor and floundered like a beached fish. His coordination had totally disintegrated.

The robot sank to the floor, loose-limbed as a marionette. Andrea grabbed a towel and went down to the gym.

The dreg lay inside, trembling and twitching. Blood dribbled from his mouth. *Petit mal?* Was he an epileptic? Was that the secret he was guarding so jealously?

Andrea approached him and knelt down. His wires were totally stripped; he was only semi-conscious. Andrea said his name.

He blinked and looked blearily up at her. Then he sat up with difficulty and wiped the blood from his mouth.

Andrea dropped the towel into his lap.

"Who were you trying to kill?" she asked. "The robot, or yourself?"

He shot her a veiled look. "Neither," he said indistinctly, and dabbed at his split lip. "Thanks for shutting that thing off. I thought I was about to get my screens cleared."

"You nearly did." But Andrea was in no mood to lecture him. She sat down beside him and propped her arms on her knees. Then she burst out laughing.

"What a pair of wipes, eh? I just totally slagged a simulation and got trashed by one of the simplest tricks in the book, and you nearly kill yourself fighting a stupid machine."

"I needed to work off some energy," he said simply. Andrea grinned at him.

"You did that. Come on." She stood and offered him a hand. "Why don't you clean up? We can go get something to eat and lick our wounds."

Jason grinned ruefully and took her hand. "You're on, Colleague."

Chapter 10

"I'm okay, really," Jason said.

They sat in wicker-style chairs at a low, glass table in the senior lounge module. Jason had chosen a table at the edge of the cool, green gardens that wandered away into the dimness. High overhead, through the plasteen dome, globular modules were stacked. Beyond and around them brilliant stars, asteroids, moved slowly across the backdrop of distant, true suns. Rising above the trees' silhouettes was the dark, spoked wheel of the old Collegium. The distant sun moved between the spokes of the old school.

Andrea ran her finger across the rim of her glass and studied Jason. He had cleaned up and did not look nearly so ravaged as he had. His hair was a tangle of damp curls, and the flesh around his eye was yellowing; he'd have a real shiner by morning. Then she glanced at her chronometer. Two and a half hours; Linc would need a definite answer before twenty-three 'oh.

No family to turn to, if I stay. I'll be alone, perhaps in the midst of a savage war. How can I stay? But I've wanted to be a pilot so badly, for so long, and I've almost made it. If I leave I'll never have a chance to command any deep space expeditions. I'll be stuck on a backwater colony, doing grunt work for the rest of my life. How can I go?

The thought made her heart ache. Jason was regarding her; she shrugged.

"It's up to you. I still think you should be checked for broken ribs, though."

He shook his head absently and leaned back to stare at the stars. "I'm all right."

"Who were you fighting in there, really?" Andrea asked. "There was murder in your eyes."

He gave her a look, raised his eyebrows. A rueful smile played across his mouth. "I hate losing to a machine."

Andrea frowned. "What are you so afraid I'll find out? I'm not a wolf, Jason. I could be an ally."

The look in his eyes was hooded. "What makes you think I have some dark secret, anyway? I'm just an ordinary dreg."

"No. You're more than that. There's something . . . I can't track it; I don't know enough." She sighed. "Frankly, Jason, you're like no other dreg I've ever seen. I watched you fighting in the gym — I watched you during the candy tests. I get the feeling you could be moved ahead a year or two and still perform at the top of your class. You're a natural. There's no doubt in my mind that you'll be valedictorian of your class."

Jason started and stared at her. Angry — or

frightened? she wondered. Then he took a long swallow of his drink. "Nothing so mysterious about that. I've got talent." Though he smiled, his voice sounded bitter. Then he gave her a quizzical look. "But enough about me. Let's talk about you. For instance, why did a talented pilot like you, prov-valley of your class, trash a sim? What ghosts are tracking you?"

"Hmmph. Change of subject. Okay, I'll stop asking questions." She leveled a finger at him. "But I won't stop trying to figure you out, dreggie."

He gazed at her, eyebrows raised.

"Now who's being evasive?" he asked. She shot him a dark look. He shrugged with a smile and propped his elbows over the back of the chair. "I won't press, if you don't want to talk about it. But if you want to talk, I'm willing to listen."

Andrea looked at her chronometer again. Nineteen 'fifteen. When she looked back up at Jason, there was compassion in his eyes. She felt despair swelling in her throat.

"I have an hour and forty-five minutes," she said, "to make a decision that will determine the course of the rest of my life."

His eyebrows shot up. "That sounds ominous."

She stood. "I'm going for a walk."

"I'll come," he said.

They followed a trail into the trees, side by side. Andrea glanced at Jason; he did not speak or even look at her.

Artificial breezes caressed her cheeks and

teased her hair. She lifted her face and gazed upward at the stars.

"Where is 40 Eridani II?"

He followed her gaze upward.

"Near Orion," he replied and squinted at the constellations above their heads. He pointed abruptly. "There — see that star beneath the Hunter's feet? Omicron 2 Eridani, more fondly known as *Al-Qaid*."

Andrea cast him a querying look. " 'Piece of the Eggshell.' Another of its names," he explained. "Omicron I Eridani, to the left over there, was known as *Beid*, 'the Egg,' by ancient Arabic astronomers. So naturally Omicron 2 Eridani was a piece of the eggshell. It has several names . . . Omicron 2 Eridani, 40 Eridani, *Al-Qaid*. All in all, a much more interesting star system than Omicron 1."

Andrea looked at the star he had pointed to. It was an ordinary looking star, white and perhaps a magnitude of three or so. Very near it, between it and Omicron I Eridani, was a much dimmer white star. "I remember reading about it," she said. "It's a double sun system."

Jason shook his head, grinning. "A triple sun system. Omicron 2 Eridani is the main sequence star, and in orbit about it at 400 a.u. is a mated red and white dwarf pair. The red dwarf is too dim to see from here without binocs or a telescope. From the colony planet, you can see both dwarves even during the day. The planet's south pole points toward them, so they look like they circle each other. We call them the Monkey and the Weasel."

The distance was mind-boggling, as was the travel time. It was hard for Andrea to imagine what it must be like for Jason, Linc, and others who traveled between the stars. To age only a few months or a year, and return to find that twenty, thirty, or as many as a hundred years had passed in that short time. No wonder her parents were not particularly overjoyed that she wanted to get into deep-space exploration.

She glanced at Jason again. He was gazing at her.

"So how about it? Are you going to tell me why you keep frowning and checking the time?"

Andrea lifted a shoulder. "You don't trust me. Why should I spill my guts to you?"

He was silent a moment. "I . . . do have specific reasons for keeping to myself, you know." He gave her a look. "I wish I could talk about it. I really do."

Andrea was skeptical. "Right."

His expression was reluctant. "It's an old and unpleasant story, Andrea. You have no idea how old and unpleasant." He exhaled. "If it weren't for Sssrei, . . ." then his voice tapered off.

"Sssrei?"

"My Shenn friend. The little alien."

Andrea gave him a curious glance. "I didn't knew they were called Shenn." She paused and nodded to herself. "So your attachment to it is personal and not religious. That makes sense."

His answering smile was a little chagrined. "I knew from the beginning you were too perceptive for my own good. Yeah. Sssrei is a friend. My only friend, really."

"Hmmm. That's pretty weird, for your only friend to be an alien animal," Andrea remarked.

He gave her a considering look, then seemed to reach some kind of decision. "Sssrei isn't an animal," he said. At her expression, he added, "They're sentient, the Shenn."

"Why do I have this feeling you're slagging me again?" she asked dryly. He winced.

"I guess I deserved that. But this time I'm being honest. I know how preposterous this sounds, but it's true. Sssrei's race is highly intelligent and technologically advanced. I'm not slagging you."

Andrea gave him a look, torn between incredulity and a desire to believe him. "How does it happen," she asked, "that you're the only human in existence that knows this?"

"That's another really long story. Besides," he gave her a sidelong glance, "if you knew something too incredible to be easily believed, would you be more likely to tell people the truth, or a believable lie? You obviously won't believe anything I tell you; can you blame me for being unwilling to tell you anything?"

"I just wish you'd stop being so slagging obscure," she replied. "Can you blame me for being suspicious, when you're so full of contradictions and lies?"

He said nothing. They walked along in silence for a long while. Finally they neared the edge of the garden and sat down on a bench. Billions of miles of cold, sterile space fell away from them, only a meter from their feet.

When Andrea looked at Jason again, he was gazing intently at her. He glanced away, embarrassed, and rested his chin on his palm.

"It's difficult," he said finally, "to know whom I can trust. Everything used to be a game. In a way. And then," he went on with obvious effort, "it all went bad, and I wanted to die. I thought I had nothing to live for. Then I found Sssrei. It gave me a reason to live, I guess you could say." He gave her a penetrating glance. "If I told you the details you simply wouldn't, couldn't believe them. So, I can't tell you . . . whatever it is I can't tell you." He paused. "But believe me, I wish I could. You're the first person in a long time I've felt I could trust."

Andrea nodded and looked away from him. She folded her legs and pulled them up. "Okay," she said. "I don't understand what you're talking about, but I'll believe you. Your alien is sentient."

She glanced at her chronometer again and fought down a wave of anxiety. Thirty-five minutes. Linc was probably looking for her right now.

She bent her head. I should go, she thought. At least I'll be safe on Centauri V. And maybe there'll be other opportunities to make a career for myself and eventually get into deep space exploration. Maybe.

"Jason," she said tentatively. He was looking at her. "If you were presented with a situation," she said, "where you had to make a choice, and both choices were rotten, what would you do?"

He laughed suddenly. "I'd love to answer that but I haven't got a clue to what you're talking about."

"It's like this." Andrea folded her hands and pressed them to her lips. "I got a whisper chip from my parents on Europa last week. They've gotten approval to join a burrowing project on Proxima Centauri, and they want me to join them. I have thirty-two minutes to decide whether I want to go, or stay here and take my chances with the war."

Jason appeared thoughtful. "If you go, then you have to give up your career as a pilot, possibly for good."

Andrea nodded, swallowed hard. "And if I stay and there's a war, I'll probably end up fighting in it. Which I don't want to do."

"And you might die," Jason said. She nodded again.

"Which I also don't want to do," she agreed and exchanged a brief, painful smile with Jason. "If it weren't for the war, I could apply with a corporation like Long Strides or Toshiba and get into a xenological expedition, but they're both Earth-based firms, and if the war starts I won't have a choice, I'll have to fight for the Commonwealth against Earth. And frankly, the idea of vaporizing people and wiping out entire cities doesn't appeal to me. I'll fight if I have to, because I think the E.A. is trying to tyrannize us and we have the right to our independence. But I don't want to."

She dug at her hair with her hands. "I don't know," she sighed. "I don't know. Maybe I should just take the easy way out, go to Proxima Centauri, and get a technical appointment."

Jason touched her hair; she looked up at him. He gathered her into his arms with a crooked smile. Andrea said nothing; her heart was pounding. She did not trust herself to speak.

"For my own sake," he said, "I hope you decide to stay."

Then he leaned forward and kissed her, gently, on the lips. Andrea drew back; his smile was quizzical and tender.

He's a dreg, she thought. I shouldn't be letting this happen. If word got around. . . .

She realized, then, that she did not really care what people thought. That surprised her. She frowned slightly and laid her head on his chest.

"You sure know how to complicate my life," she said.

He lay his cheek against her head and played with a lock of her hair. She could hear the smile in his voice. "That was the idea."

She wrapped her arms around his chest and lifted her face to meet his gaze.

"I think I'm going to go," she said. "If I stay I'll probably never see my family again; I'll have no money and no relatives to turn to if we lose the war. I'll have nothing except a career as a professional soldier, a mercenary, and I'll probably end up dead or a prisoner of war. I can't take that chance. It's too big a risk."

Jason's eyes narrowed. She noticed how long and dark his lashes were and how his eyes had a ring of amber around the irises. She also saw the tiny scars around his nose and eyebrows — he had had extensive plastic surgery. The realization distracted her, and also shocked her.

Jason said, "There might not be a war." His voice had meaningful undertones she did not understand; she shrugged his words off.

"At this point you're about the only person who believes that."

"Maybe," he said, "I have good reason to be."

She straightened and gazed at him suspiciously. "What does that mean?"

Instead of answering, though, he smiled again and pulled her back, gave her a longer, deeper kiss. Andrea hesitated, then pulled free and stood. She looked at him for a long moment without speaking.

Andrea said, "Good-bye, Jason," and walked away.

Chapter 11

She found Dave Turin down the hall from her dorm. He was pacing back and forth, looking pensive. Andrea stopped in her tracks and drew a breath to steady herself. She did not want to make this decision.

Not that hard. Just say, *I'm going*. I'm going, she thought. The words made her feel strange, numb. She looked around at the pearl-colored walls. Well, at least she wouldn't have to say good-bye to everyone. It would be too painful. But she would leave a note for Vic and the Weasel.

She laughed. The only cadet who knew she was leaving was some weird dreg she hardly knew, to whom she was attracted but couldn't decide if she liked, and whom she would never see again. Ironic.

Andrea started forward again. Linc spotted her and strode swiftly toward her.

"Andy! I've been looking for you all day."

She could not bring herself to meet her old friend's gaze.

"I'm sorry I didn't come to you earlier, Linc."

Nervously, she pulled her hair back and tied it into a swift knot. Linc's gaze was piercing.

"Well, what's it going to be, kid? If we want to hit the window, we need to leave in fifteen minutes, max."

She said, softly, "I'm going."

He nodded. "Then get your things. I'll meet you in the launch bay."

He turned to go.

"Linc. . . ."

The pilot turned back.

"Am I making the wrong decision?"

He walked back and studied her. "Do you want me to play Devil's advocate?"

Andrea nodded.

"Well, then." He slipped his thumbs into his pockets. "I'll make it fast, since we're rushed for time. I'd say you've taken the safe way out and that you're probably going to regret it."

She gaped at him, speechless. He nodded at her expression. "I know, you assumed I was in favor of your joining your family. I'm not, and I tried to argue your parents out of offering to take you."

"Why?" she managed to say. He looked severe.

"I don't condemn your parents for going, Andrea. They could make a real contribution to the Centauri project, and quite frankly, so could you. But your real gift is as a pilot, and a xenogeologist.

"Your parents are bankrupting themselves to make this trip. Centauri V won't be profitable for years. They'll be stuck there with no opportunity to return, nor do anything but work themselves to exhaustion making the colony a success, for a very long time. If you go, you'll be in the same hole."

Some students walked past and stopped to talk outside a nearby door. Linc gave them a glance, then took Andrea's arm and led her down the hall. Once they were alone he continued, "I can't tell you what the right decision is, Andy. If you stay, you're taking a big risk. But in the first place, there may not be a war. Everyone will be better off if the E.A. and the Commonwealth reach an agreement; only the most shortsighted on both sides deny that. And in the second place, even if there is a war, it won't last forever. And when it's over your talents will be desperately needed. You'll be able to write your own ticket. You'll easily be able to save the money to visit your family if you hit it as big as I suspect you will. So it's not as if you'll never see them again.

"I think," he finished frankly, "that you are perfectly capable of making your own way in the world." Then he spread his hands. "But it is a big risk, and I could be wrong."

"Linc," Andrea's voice broke. She fought down tears. "I don't want to die, and I don't want to kill."

"So?" He shrugged. "You'll get some very attractive offers to be a fighter pilot. That doesn't mean you have to take them. I wouldn't be surprised if Collegium makes you an offer, in which case you'll be able to stay out of the war and still stay insystem. And if not, there'll be a number of neutral enclaves that'll want pilots. But I'll give you odds Collegium will ask you to stay on in a professional capacity."

She gave him a troubled glance. "That's possible, I suppose. But I think the Hammer is expecting trouble. A couple of weeks ago I saw faxes on his desk having to do with fighting. I think he expects us to get involved in the war."

"The Hammer? Oh. Tram." He frowned. "Well, it's possible, I suppose. But not very likely. That's just Tram, though. He was always a bit paranoid, even back when we were in school."

Andrea stared at him. Tram? Senior Admin Trammerden. The Hammer.

Linc noticed the intensity of her stare. "What is it?" he asked. She did not answer.

Jason Stiletto had a grudge. Against Senior Administrator Jon Trammerden.

It was absolutely impossible. Jason had only just arrived from a colony almost sixteen light-years away. There was no way they could know each other. All of Trammerden's exploits, before his appointment, had been insystem. If Jason had been to Sol before, the round trip to Eridani and back again would have taken about thirty-two years, which meant that when Jason was here the first time Trammerden would have only been a toddler.

It was impossible. Why did it make so much sense?

Linc was still eyeing her. "Six minutes, Andrea, or your decision's made for you. Grab your duffel bag now, or forget it."

Andrea thought for a moment. The puzzle that was Jason Stiletto did not really matter, not if she were going. Do I really want to go? There won't be any changing my mind.

She took a deep breath and met Linc's gaze. "I'm staying. I'll find some way to stay out of the war, if I can. I can't give up my dream."

He broke into a smile. "Brave choice. I'm with you, Colleague."

She drew a shaky breath and said, smiling back, "Now, let's go to the senior lounge and talk a whole lot."

"Fair enough."

In the lounge, they picked a table and sat down. A server robot hovered near them.

"May I take your orders?" it said.

Linc smiled at Andrea, his eyes shining. "This calls for a celebration. What'll you have, Colleague? My treat."

Andrea considered. "A Topknot, I think."

"Make that two." After Linc tossed a coin onto the server's flat surface, its mechanical arms extended toward them two frosted glasses with barber-pole-striped straws and paper parasols, filled with iced green liquid. Andrea drew on the straw. The icy liquid trickled down her throat. She sat back, thinking.

"When did you graduate, Linc?" she asked. "2088, right?"

"Yeah. Why?"

"Just thinking." She took another sip. "Were you in the same class as Admin Trammerden?"

"Uh-uh. A year behind. We're not friends, if that's what you're wondering. Tram wasn't too easy to get along with. Brilliant pilot, though. Valley of his class, though he wouldn't have been if MacLeod hadn't gotten wiped across the face of a planetoid."

Andrea leaned forward. "MacLeod?"

"Jason MacLeod. An Eridani kid. Now Mac-Leod, there was a prodigy. He was even younger than most of the juniors. He started out in my class, but his performance was so good they put him up a year."

Andrea feigned only mild interest, but her pulse had quickened. Jason MacLeod. Jason. "Oh really? How did he get wiped?"

Linc's gaze grew a little distant. "It was tragic. A fluke. Both his normal and emergency navigational computers went down during graduation exercises. You know Dead Man's Run?" Andrea nodded wordlessly. "We called it the Road to Glory. You know what a turn it is to navigate in."

Andrea winced sympathetically. That couldn't be her Jason, no one would survive a collision in Dead Man's Run. "Then he died."

"Nope. That was the sad part, in a way. The med teams found him and kept him alive, pieced him back together. Sent him back to 40 Eridani II in an ice chest."

"Surely they could give him regeneration and therapy, then. . . ."

"Ye . . . e . . . s," Linc replied slowly and twirled his straw, scraping the frost from the inside of his glass. "I imagine they did. I'm sure he's leading a relatively normal life now. But with the brain and nerve damage he suffered, there was no way he could ever pilot a craft again." He paused. "I think about Mac-Leod occasionally. Oh well." He grinned. "Don't get me reminiscing — I'll bore you to a stupor."

Andrea took another sip, without tasting it. "No, I'm quite interested. What did this Jason look like?"

"Now you're really testing my memory," he said with a laugh. Then his eyes narrowed to slits. "Rather small, but muscular, wiry, I guess you'd say. Big nose. He reminded me a bit of a cat. The way he walked, you know, and the way he stared people down. I may be remembering wrong, though. It's been almost eleven years for me."

"And nineteen years, stay-time," Andrea murmured. Enough time for a one-way trip, and a couple years of therapy. It was Jason. She was certain. But he couldn't be back in Sol for another fifteen years, even if he had turned around and come straight back. How could it be him?

If I told you, you wouldn't believe me.

How did you do it, Jason? she wondered. How did you get back here from Eridani without paying your respects to stay-time, and why are you out to get Trammerden? Then she shook her head. It simply couldn't be.

She finished her drink. "Well, I'd better get to bed; I've got a full schedule tomorrow." She rested a hand on Linc's shoulder. "Thanks for everything, Linc."

Jason sat at the little table next to his bed,

doodling on an old printout. There had to be some way ... some way to get at Tram's private files. If only Sssrei had some knowledge of computers, he thought. Or could pick the passwords out of Tram's head. But Sssrei had made it quite clear that the only human mind it could read was Jason's. It could wipe out the man's mind, if its life were gravely threatened, but Jason did not want to destroy Trammerden's mind. He wanted Tram to know who had ruined him, and why.

So Jason needed information: information Trammerden kept well protected. Jason was deadlocked. Unless ... unless, he thought suddenly, Tram kept hard copies of evidence in his quarters. Jason was willing to bet he did.

It was worth a try. It was his only hope. Unbelievably risky, but Jason was not about to give up now. Tomorrow night, he thought, I'll break in then. That'll give me the afternoon after classes to find out what I can about the layout of his quarters. Might as well not drag this out.

The thought made his stomach knot. If he discovers me I'm wiped for real and good. Given a choice between that and utter defeat, though, Jason reflected, I'll take the risk. His lips pulled back across his teeth. If he discovers me, it'll be almost worth it just to see the look on his face when he realizes who has broken into his quarters.

"Hey dreg."

Jason started and looked over his shoulder at

the senior who bunked next to him. He was glaring blearily at Jason.

"We had sims all day and we've got more tomorrow. Don't you believe in sleep?"

There were muffled snarls of agreement from around the darkened room. With a sigh, Jason flipped off his little desk lamp. His dormmates had, gradually and grudgingly, come to respect him. He had mediated, both with words and fists, in several fights among the testy seniors. The combination of his sense of fairness and his ferocity had won them over, and even Simon and his group were coming around.

He remembered how edgy and nervous he had been before his finals. He really should not be keeping them awake.

Jason stripped and climbed into bed.

"Sssrei?"

The alien's thoughts filled his mind, querying.

"Do you feel hungry or cramped? I can take you out tomorrow if you want to stretch your, um, spikes. You must be terribly bored."

Amusement answered him. "Jason-human, I have spent much of my time riding within your mind, when you are within range. I have never been so mobile in my life. I like bonding with humans. I must recommend to my people when we get back that they all nearly die and be rescued by you."

A reluctant smile twisted Jason's lips. "Not funny, Sssrei. I nearly dropped you."

"Ah, but you didn't drop me. And look at what a marvelous experience I've gained as a result!"

Jason chuckled softly and started to drift off to sleep.

"Jason?"

"Hmmm?" he thought sleepily.

"I have finally found a good justification to my people for helping you in your vendetta."

Jason was abruptly awake, staring at the darkness. "Have you?"

"Yes," it thought complacently. "I saw in your mind what your people are like. Often they are . . . not entirely trustworthy. My people can protect themselves against humans, as you have guessed, but it occurs to me that if you can rout this evil human, Trammerden, with my help, perhaps in their gratitude your people will be more inclined to bargain with us. This will reduce the possibility of violence or disappointment."

"Faster-than-light travel is a pretty powerful bargaining tool, friend," Jason replied. "Don't worry, they'll give a fortune for the convolver. And your people will never know about this sidetrack I've taken you on, unless you want them to. You won't be in danger from my people or yours. Your people will get what they need. You'll have your 'companions.' I'll see to it."

"It is a good rationale, though, is it not?" the alien thought. There was the distinct air of a plea in its thought-tone.

"Outstanding. And true, if a little disturbing," Jason thought, "that we humans are so obviously untrustworthy."

"If you were telepaths as my people are, you'd be much more reliable as a species."

Jason glowered toward the foot of his bed. "Stop being smug and go to sleep."

"Shenn don't sleep," Sssrei rejoined. With a grunt, Jason covered his head with his pillow. It was a futile gesture.

"Jason?"

He stifled a groan. "What?"

"I liked kissing the Andrea-human. I think you should do it some more."

Outraged embarrassment made him sit bolt upright. "You eavesdropped on that?"

"I can't help it, Jason," the alien said contritely, "when you are near me I am within your thoughts. I . . . found the exchange very pleasant. Among my people there is no analog."

Jason lay back down, fuming. In the future he would have to make sure he was a goodly distance from the dorm beforehand. . . .

"Don't count on any more thrills with Andrea," he thought. "She's probably on her way to Europa by now." He found the thought depressing. "By the way . . . what is your range, Sssrei?"

"I am uncertain." It thought for a moment. "When you attend your calculus class I am barely with you, but directly afterwards you fade away and I am alone. It is very lonely when you are not with me," it added wistfully.

Jason did a quick calculation. That was roughly half a kilometer, a quarter of the way across Collegium. He would bear that distance in mind.

Chapter 12

The final question on the Field Theory test was on the console before Jason. He read the problem. It was a simple one:

THE TAU CETI STAR SYSTEM IS APPROXIMATELY ELEVEN LIGHT-YEARS FROM THE SOL STAR SYSTEM. FOR A CRUISER TRAVELING FROM SOL TO TAU CETI AT 98% OF THE SPEED OF LIGHT, CALCULATE:

(A) HOW LONG THE SHIP TAKES TO REACH TAU CETI, STATIONARY TIME. (TS)

(B) HOW MUCH TIME PASSES FOR THE PASSENGERS ABOARD THE SHIP. (TD)

EQUATIONS:___

ASSUMPTIONS:

CALCULATIONS:

A space for the answers was at the bottom of the screen.

Jason felt Omungo staring at him and looked up. The Kenyan expatriot sat at the front of the classroom, rocking his chair and watching Jason with a hard glitter in his eyes. The other dreggies were shifting in their seats, casting desperate looks around the room, and scribbling frantically on scratch paper.

Omungo's been looking at my answers, Jason realized with panic. Although Jason had made sure to let a couple of errors creep into his calculations, he would still get a very high score. I think it's time, he reflected, to wipe a problem totally.

The equation he needed was,

$$Ts = Td \sqrt{\frac{1}{1 - v^2/c^2}}$$

where Ts was stay-time, the amount of time that passed for people who were "stationary," and Td was dial-time, the time that passed for people going close to the speed of light — dilated time. The variable v was the velocity of the ship and c was the speed of light.

Jason could pretty much do the calculations in his head now, and Omungo had chosen a problem that was easily figured. Ts, stay-time, was simply the distance traveled divided by the ship's velocity.

$$Ts = \frac{distance}{ship\ velocity}$$

The distance from Sol to Tau Ceti was eleven light-years, and the ship velocity was 0.98 times the speed of light. Light, obviously, traveled at one light-year per year. So the ship would travel 0.98 light-years per year. So,

$$Ts = \frac{11 \text{ light-years}}{0.98 \text{ light-years/year}}$$

Ts came out to be about eleven-point-two years. It would take eleven years and just under three months, stay-time, for a ship to get to Tau Ceti, if it traveled at 98% of the speed of light.

Since v was 0.98 light-years per year and c was one light-year per year,

$$\frac{v^2}{c^2} = \frac{(0.98)(0.98)}{(1)(1)} = \frac{0.96}{1} = 0.96$$

So the fraction $\dfrac{1}{\left(1 - \dfrac{v^2}{c^2}\right)}$ came out to be

$1/(0.04)$, or twenty-five. And the square root of twenty-five was, quite neatly, five. Stay-time would be five times dial-time.

So dial-time was one-fifth of stay-time. One-fifth of eleven-point-two years, or about two years and three months, would go by for the passengers in the ship, during the eleven years and three months that went by for the "stationary" universe.

When the ship got back to Sol, they would have aged only four and a half years while more than twenty-two years would have passed for the people back home. A young woman who had traveled on that ship would be the same age as her son had become. Her husband would be close to twice her age; her parents would probably be dead.

Word problem. If, Jason thought, a boy came from his home world around 40 Eridani II to Sol in a ship traveling 99.99% of the speed of light, stayed three years, and went back, about thirty-six years would have passed for the people back home while only four had passed for him.

His parents would be dead, his brothers and sisters would have grown up and had families and lives of their own — they would be completely different from the children he had played and fought with. His old friends would be strangers. He would have been completely forgotten. The buildings, the streets — everything — would be changed; he would be an alien among his own people.

That boy would have cheated time, but the price would have had to be paid on his return . . . C.O.D.

And if that boy came back in shame and defeat, a physical and emotional cripple, no one would want to remember him. They would look at him with disgust and pity and say to each other: *There's the kid they scraped money together for to send to Collegium. He was a real whiz.*

Ain't it a shame.

That kid would have nothing to live for. His

life would have become an endless succession of humiliation and pain, of operations, skin grafts, and regeneration — and, after all this, the kid would be cheerfully informed that he could get a land grant and become a homesteader.

That kid would probably decide that it would be better to go out in a blaze of glory avenging himself on the one who had done this to him than to live out a long, bitter life filled with drudgery and self-hatred.

But again, time would exact its price. He could afford to return to Sol to ruin his betrayer; his parents would have left him his inheritance in a trust fund. He could reach Sol again in about another six months, dial-time — but by then the one who had almost killed him, who had destroyed his life, would be old or even dead, after having lived a very long and fulfilling life. Stay-time wouldn't wait for the kid to have his revenge.

While that kid was traveling close to the speed of light, in dial-time, stay-time would be consuming the universe around him, aging it at a greatly accelerated rate. Changing it beyond recognition.

Unless there were a way to travel faster than the speed of light. To weave a path — convolve — along and within the edges of intersecting universes. To cheat stay-time without its knowledge. To travel in rogue-time.

There were only a few minutes left for the test. Jason hurriedly calculated the wrong numbers for Ts and Td, entered them at the bottom of the page, and pressed RETURN. The screen cleared.

The whistle sounded, and students began to talk among themselves. Jason tossed his texts into his satchel and stood; as he passed Omungo's desk, the man motioned him over. He stopped, apprehensive. The other students filed past him.

Omungo was studying his screen.

"Stupid mistake on that last problem, Stiletto. You forgot to take the square root of the ratio."

"I guess I was in a hurry."

Omungo eyed him. "I guess you were. You raced through the beginning of the test like there was no tomorrow, and then sat in your chair daydreaming for ten minutes before you could be bothered to start the last problem." He frowned forbiddingly at Jason.

"The problems on that test came straight out of the sophomore finals, Stiletto. I gave this exam," he tapped the screen with an enormous fingernail, "to test your limits, in particular. You're no dreg."

Jason stared at him, frozen. Outside the class he could hear the murmur and footfalls of students going to class. Omungo and he stared at each other. I'm done for, he thought. They've found me out.

Omungo lowered his eyes to the papers on his desk. "I've checked your scores in your other classes. Same high marks, punctuated by occasional carelessness. Nonetheless, outstanding marks. You should be put up, Stiletto. I'm putting your name before the Council to be promoted to junior next semester."

Jason's breath escaped in a hiss of relief. It was followed quickly by a rush of panic. Trammerden would have to approve it before the Council ever saw Omungo's proposal. Carefully, he said, "Thank you, sir, but I'm sure you overestimate my abilities. I . . . don't want to be put forward. I'm quite comfortable where I am."

"No doubt," Omungo said sarcastically. His black eyes flashed at Jason. "You'd love it if you could waltz your way through here, wouldn't you? But you aren't here to be comfortable. You're here to be pushed to your limits, to realize your full capacity. You've already shown evidence of inexcusable laziness. If you drag along this way you'll end up a second-rate pilot who thinks he's better than anyone else."

Omungo leveled a finger at him. "If you're going to think you're better than anyone else, dreg, you'd better be. Otherwise someone who is better than you is going to come along and wipe your screens."

He brushed aside Jason's protest. "End of discussion. It's decided."

"But sir. . . ."

Omungo silenced him with a look. "You'll be late for your next class, cadet."

Jason stalked out of the room, fuming.

The Eridanian's little yacht sat in the dry dock bay, dwarfed by the several giant insystem craft around it. Andrea had wandered among the cruisers and freighters for almost ten minutes before she found the yacht. Now she stood a short distance away, eyeing it.

The yacht, an old model Miranda 9Y5, was a dull gray tetrahedron of titanium and epoxy, with six posterior nozzles, a transparent nose and some evidence of particle scoring along the sides. The model and serial numbers on the airlock door were faded and peeling, but the vessel's name, *Blaze'a'Glory*, was in large new red letters along the body, underscored by a flaming yellow and orange meteor.

The old Miranda yachts had simple magnetic locks, so Jason's ship should be easy to break into. Andrea looked around; no one was in sight. The single tech on duty was near the bay entrance. Andrea took out her palm-sized microscanner and magneto-key lattice and approached the door of the yacht.

She attached the key's lead to the microscanner and turned on the decoder. Seconds later a series of hollow clanks came from within the airlock mechanism, and the door whispered open. Andrea glanced around again, stepped inside the airlock, and closed the door behind her.

The lock's inner door opened into the yacht lounge. A low couch encircled the room, and a projection globe hung above the table against the far wall. The door to her right led to the cockpit; Andrea did not bother with that. The item she sought, if it existed, would be in the engine room.

To her left, against the curved lounge wall, were three doors. The one she wanted would be the middle one; the other two were doubtless living quarters.

She touched the panel by the door and the door slid open to reveal a short hall which ended in snaking pipes and machinery. Cautiously, looking for infrared alarms, she entered the engine room.

Almost half an hour later, Andrea propped herself against one of the power chutes, frustrated. She had been so sure . . . but the yacht's drive was a standard antimatter engine with no alterations or anything out of the ordinary.

Well, it had been a wild theory anyhow, to think that an Eridani colonist could somehow develop a faster-than-light means of propulsion. But that was the only way Jason MacLeod could have reached 40 Eridani II, which she had verified that he had, and be back at Sol so quickly.

All of Andrea's investigation so far had led her to believe that Stiletto and MacLeod were one and the same. But he simply could not be back so soon after he had left.

Andrea stood with a sigh. Slag Stiletto. She had graduation to worry about. The written tests started tomorrow, and exercises were scheduled three days later. Jason MacLeod — if that's who he was — could wait till after graduation.

She walked back out to the lounge and stared at the airlock door in alarm — she saw movement through its window.

Andrea ducked back into the corridor before

the door closed. Then she pressed her ear against the door and listened; she could hear footsteps and Jason's voice. The footsteps grew nearer — she retreated into the engine room and ducked under the chutes, heading toward the back where the ship's force field generator was located.

She paused for an instant at the steel-blue generator. An octopuslike machine hung on the generator's trunk like a parasite. Andrea had never seen anything like it. She ducked around the field generator and studied the contraption at close hand.

The machine was part metal and part silica; its interior had facets and planes that caught light and confused the eye — Andrea had the sense, staring into the device, that she was looking into infinity.

FTL. Not a drive, but a modified energy field for faster than light travel? Andrea nodded thoughtfully. It could be.

She looked back toward the corridor. Apparently Jason was not coming into the engine room right away, but he might eventually, so it would be wise to get out of the ship right now.

She went back to the lounge door and listened. Nothing. Here goes, she thought, and opened the door. The lounge was empty. Across the room, the cockpit door was open. Jason's voice came from there; she could see the back of his head and his hands on the controls of the ship computer. Who was he talking to? She saw no one else in the cockpit.

Quietly, she moved closer, pressing herself against the wall.

". . . yeah, it's risky. The layout files might be booby-trapped with alarms, too. I doubt we'll trigger any of them, though. I haven't found any evidence that he used his super-security software on anything but the defense systems and his personal files, and this intruder program of mine knows how to slip past the usual alarms." He was quiet a moment. "There! It got through!"

Andrea risked a look into the cockpit. Jason was studying something on a holographic projection. Andrea craned her neck — the holo seemed to be a floor plan of some kind. She hid behind the door as Jason moved into full view.

After a few moments of silence, Jason said, "I don't think so. Look. If he had a safe there he would have to reroute the fire extinguishing lines. No, he'd put it someplace that wouldn't require any rewiring or piping — otherwise he'd have to let others in on its existence and location. Which isn't his style at all."

There was more silence; Andrea chanced another peek. He *had* to be talking to someone.

He was still studying the projection. Then he pointed. "You mean there? . . . Hmm. Possibly, but it's awfully close to the power plates. What about there, behind the desk?" He was silent. "Okay, then, we'll try both of them. Now, let's get a hard copy and get out of the system, before someone detects our intrusion."

Andrea turned and headed quietly for the airlock. She had heard enough.

Jason, behind her, said to his invisible companion, "Sure, it's safe enough in here. I'll join you in a minute."

She heard a scraping sound and turned. The little alien was rolling into the room on a double row of spikes that extended and retracted along the circumference of its body. Then it stopped, and its meter-long fibers arced toward her, as though bending before a breeze. A number of thoughts raced through her mind — he had been talking to the alien, and it had talked back. Telepathy, or something like it.

Highly intelligent . . . technologically advanced. The alien had given Jason FTL.

"Jason, I think you'd better come out here. We have a visitor."

Jason's hands froze over the keys. "What?"

He shot to his feet and propelled himself into the lounge. Andrea stood at the airlock door, her head cocked at Sssrei. She had an odd expression on her face. Jason swallowed the lump of panic in his throat and attempted indignation.

"Andrea, what are you doing here?"

"Jason MacLeod," she said, giving him a slow smile.

He went numb. She knew everything.

She crossed over to the couch and sat down. "I came here," she said, "to check your engines in order to verify a theory I had. I got more than I bargained for."

Jason joined her on the couch and put a look of sincere perplexity on his face. "You've got me confused."

She smiled at him. "No, I've got you scared. You're masking it beautifully, though. All that therapy on 40 Eridani II on top of your Collegium training must have given you amazing self-control."

Jason felt as though he had been slugged in the stomach. Think, MacLeod, there has to be some way out of this. He caught a glimpse of Sssrei as it rolled toward them, its optic filaments swaying back and forth to study them.

Andrea laughed. "You're good, Colleague. You had me going in circles, and I'm no dummy."

"I really haven't got a clue to what you mean," Jason said. His mouth had gone dry, but he smiled into her penetrating gaze. "What are you talking about?"

She shrugged at him with a crooked smile and leaned back into her locked fingers. "What is that contraption hooked up to your force field, anyway? I couldn't make head nor tail of it."

He stiffened in outrage. "How dare you snoop around my ship?"

"Relax! I didn't touch it," she assured him. "I told you — I just wanted to verify a theory. Last night I began to suspect who you were, so after prep runs today I did some checking." She ticked off facts on her fingers. "One Jason MacLeod, critically injured during exercises on September 14, 2087, arrived on 40 Eridani II on October 28, 2103. Three years ago. Hospital records show he was a patient for nineteen months, I believe it was. Fizz stats of this Jason MacLeod match yours. I owe a big one to Tolyer and computer networking for all that, let me tell you." She regarded him for a moment.

"So I asked myself, how could this Jason MacLeod get back to Sol only fifteen months after he left a hospital on 40 Eridani II? The soonest he should be able to get here was sometime in May of 2121."

Jason spread his hands. "Obviously the records were confused." He raised an eyebrow at her. "Jason is a common name on Eridani, you know. And records get confused all the time, especially back home. We haven't been tagged into the tolyernet all that long."

She gazed at him narrowly. "Granted. Pretty unlikely, since hospital records show no evidence of a Jason Stiletto, but possible. But just play along with me for a minute; this should entertain you." She drew her legs up under her.

"Assuming that Jason Stiletto and Jason MacLeod are the same person, how do I get past the time factor? I know MacLeod reached Eridani after his accident. The only way he could get back here again so quickly is if he had a faster-than-light field. Something like the device back in your engine room is my guess."

"FTL is a fiction," he said stiffly. "It's impossible."

She stared at him for a long moment, then shrugged, seeming disappointed in him. "Well, you would know, I suppose. You said last night that if you told me your 'secret,' I wouldn't believe you. Well, I believe you. I know I'm right — and I know that I can't prove it; no one would believe me either." She came to her feet. "I hoped you would trust me."

Jason scoffed. "Quite a fantasy, Colleague," he remarked caustically. "Do you always create such wild histories for guys who kiss you a couple of times? I thought you were leaving, anyhow. Where do you get off picking my life apart?"

Andrea's color darkened. "Have it your way. I'll just report my findings to Senior Admin Trammerden and let him decide if you're his old colleague."

He went cold and met her eyes. He sighed, deep and long. "Dirty trick, Andrea. If I were MacLeod, that would be a really cheap shot."

"And your crack wasn't?" He said nothing.

"Well?" she asked. "If you aren't MacLeod, then you shouldn't care what I tell Trammerden. And if you are, then you'd better tell me now."

"You're going to have to tell her, Jason," Sssrei told him.

"Shut up," he snarled at the alien, and then met Andrea's gaze. She looked at him and then at Sssrei, and nodded to herself.

Jason rubbed his brow. "You've really complicated things." He hesitated for a second. "You got everything pretty much right. The convolver, the device you saw, is an FTL field."

Andrea sat back down. He filled in the details she had missed and told her how he and Sssrei had fallen in together. After he was released from the hospital on 40 Eridani II, Jason had spent a lot of time on the coast, going for long walks beneath the cliffs. Late one afternoon he had seen on a ledge directly above him a predator, a spider-like creature with mandibles of razor-sharp glass, about to make a kill. The spider creature had trapped — something, a spherical creature Jason had never seen before — in a crevice.

As Jason watched, the predator lifted its prey and locked its mandibles on it, preparing to crack its shell like a walnut. Suddenly, the spider creature tossed its prey away and began to convulse wildly, whipping its tentacles about and clacking its mandibles frenziedly.

Jason dove to catch the small spherical creature as it plummeted. As he caught it, an explosion of color and sound spread through his mind, a chaotic jumble of alien imagery and emotions. Sssrei's telepathic death-cry had blasted through Jason's barriers and activated his latent psychic abilities. An unbreakable link had been forged.

Sssrei had been on its way to the humans, to make a last desperate attempt to get through to them and find a way to save its slowly dying race. Jason and it had devised a plan — use Sssrei's superior knowledge and Jason's technical skills to build the convolver. They would prove the convolver by coming back to Sol and offer the device to the humans in exchange for biomechanical "bodies" for the Shenn.

Andrea listened with head bent and hands folded in her lap. When he had finished, she said, "That still doesn't explain what you're doing back here. You're out to get Trammerden, aren't you?"

Jason rested his arms on the back of the couch and gave her a wry smile. "Something like that."

"Because you think he sabotaged your ship, to wipe you during grad exercises."

"I don't think; I know." He leaned forward, intense. "He entered the launch bay after me, right before exercises. I had checked my backup systems thoroughly just before he went in."

She frowned. "That's not proof. Any number of things could have happened during flight to cause the malfunction. There's no way you could know. . . ."

"I know." He said it brutally. She looked at him for a moment, doubt on her face, then shook her head.

"Impossible. He wouldn't."

"I can't prove it," Jason said, standing. He picked up Sssrei. "And I'm not asking you to believe me. All I'm asking is that you trust me enough to keep quiet about this for a little while — I'll have my proof soon enough."

Andrea's gaze was apprehensive and suspicious. "What are you planning, Jason?"

He shook his head. "Uh-uh. Best you know as little as possible."

She came to her feet, gripped his arm, and gave him a piercing look. "You're not going to kill him?"

"I'm not a murderer, Andrea." He shook his arm loose. "Much as I'd like to make him suffer the way I did. No, I'm not going to kill him." I'm going to make him wish he were dead. But he did not say it. He stared at her a moment longer, and then turned away. "I have things do, Andrea," he said. "Perhaps you'd better go."

"Jason. . . ." He looked back at her. She stood with her arms at her sides. Then she passed him and opened the airlock door. "Don't do anything stupid," she said.

"I don't plan to."

She eyed him for a moment and then left. Jason turned back to Sssrei.

"Do you trust her?"

"I don't know, Sssrei." Jason turned back toward the cockpit. "I'm going to have to. If she turns drone there's not much we can do. She won't, I think." He set Sssrei down in the co-pilot seat and called up the stats for Tram's quarters, to begin decoding the lock sequence.

She won't turn drone. I hope.

Chapter 13

Linc's quarters were in one of the outermost modules, where gravity was lightest. Andrea paced the hall near his room, paused, approached his room, then thrust her hands into her jacket pockets and leaned against the wall.

To snitch or not to snitch. That was the question. If she told Linc what she had learned, she'd be a drone as surely as if she had told Trammerden himself.

Senior Admin Trammerden, the most famous pilot in the system — an attempted murderer?

Jason had been so certain. He had come an awfully long way and risked a lot on the basis of that conviction. But he had undergone a horrible, mind-twisting experience. His suspicions were not exactly reliable.

Yet his psych stats had shown a strong sense of fairness and no evidence of paranoia. He had apparently known the Hammer quite well. What if it were true?

If there were even a remote chance that Jason was right about Trammerden, and Andrea told the Senior Administrator about Jason's intent on revenge, she'd be signing Jason's death warrant for sure.

If only I knew what Jason was about to do. If I knew for certain he wasn't going to attack the Senior Administrator . . . if only he would have trusted me.

She sighed in frustration. This was getting her nowhere; she needed to know more about Trammerden and Jason MacLeod. And the one person at hand who had known them both was Linc. But he might feel compelled to go to Trammerden if she told him about Jason.

She would just have to extract a promise from him beforehand not to ask her any probing questions. She simply could not forget about this, and she would not betray Jason. Unless she found strong evidence that he was a rogue, that he meant to do Trammerden harm.

Linc seemed surprised to see her. He opened the door and she followed him into his room. He had depolarized an entire wall. Outside, drone tugs towed asteroids about, rearranging the maze called Kodiak Death. The sun, about the size of a half-pound coin, lit the hull of the old school, beyond the mazes. Andrea sat down on his bed, slipped off her boots, and folded her legs. Linc watched her closely.

"Tests start tomorrow?" he prompted. She nodded.

"That's not it, though. Linc," she sat forward and gave him an intent look. "May I ask you some questions without having to explain why I'm asking them? It's important."

He nodded slowly.

Andrea looked down at her hands. "I need to know what your old classmate MacLeod was like."

"Hmm. Odd line of questioning, my dear." At her reproving glance he grimaced. "I know — I promised not to ask. Well." He sat down at his desk and tilted the chair back. "I presume you mean what his personality was like?"

Andrea nodded.

"Easy to respect, not easy to get to know. He was driven — almost obsessive — about being the best. Tram and he were alike in that way. There were times I thought they'd kill each other."

Andrea started. Linc gave her a quizzical look and shrugged. "I can't really tell you much more than that; I didn't know MacLeod all that well. He tracked awful close to rogue, but I liked him. Which is more than I could say for Tram, frankly."

"Why?"

He paused, then shook his head. "Tram was okay, I suppose. Look, Andy, I'm uncomfortable talking about Tram like this. He wasn't an especially nice human being as a cadet, but he has done some remarkable things in the last twenty years and has really enhanced Collegium's prestige since the Council appointed him. I don't like the man, but I can appreciate what he's done. Collegium's power base has expanded dramatically since Tram took control. Also, he's virtually guaranteed Collegium's neutrality in the war."

He gave Andrea a wry smile. "So, no, I don't like Trammerden. But I appreciate what he's accomplished, whatever his motives are."

"What are his motives, then?" Andrea asked.

"Personal power." Linc said it matter-of-factly.

Andrea thought for a minute. "MacLeod's accident, back in 2087. Any possibility it might not have been an accident?"

Linc stared at her. "Where did you hear about that?"

Startled by Linc's intensity, Andrea stammered, "About what?"

He gave her a searching look. "I wish you hadn't extracted an oath of silence from me. I sure would like to know what you're tracking onto." Then he sat back, still studying her. "There were rumors that MacLeod's ship might have been tampered with. The chance that both the main and the auxiliary navigation systems would go out at the same instant is — impossibly remote. And two seniors had overheard Tram telling MacLeod that he'd make sure MacLeod didn't make valedictorian."

Then he shook his head. "But they went over the wreckage and found no evidence of tampering — and Tram had an unimpeachable alibi; every minute of his time was accounted for by the computers for six hours before the launch, before and after the techs did their final checks. MacLeod had been in the launch bay about three hours before exercises started. At the hearing they decided that he had probably sabotaged his own systems, inadvertently. So the charges against Tram were dropped." Linc paused.

Andrea nodded. Her eyes narrowed. A thorough inquiry had established that Trammerden was innocent. So Jason was wrong. Obsessed.

Considering what he had been through she could hardly blame him. But that meant he was rogue, or awfully close. And she was rogue-friend. She had not only recruited him; she had befriended him — become involved with him. Trusted him. It would destroy her career, brand her for life. She had not reported her suspicions to the admin staff. Trammerden's life might be in danger. Andrea's skin crawled with gooseflesh.

She shook her head in violent disbelief. Not Jason. He would not harm Trammerden.

She looked again at Linc, who was eyeing her.

"Did Jason . . . did MacLeod know about the inquiry?"

"Not at the time. He was in cold storage, on his way to 40 Eridani II, and in no shape to attend the hearings. He was probably notified when he got back; the inquiry records would have reached the colony shortly after he did back in 2103."

Andrea pressed her hands against her lips with a frown.

I've got to talk to Jason again, she decided. I've got to persuade him that he's wrong, that he's only going to get himself arrested if he keeps on this way. She stood and pulled her boots on. "Thanks for the information, Linc. I probably won't see you again till after graduation. . . ."

He stood, too, and gave her shoulder a squeeze. "I sure wish I knew what you're up to, kid." He walked her to the door.

"Maybe I can tell you in a few days."

"And speaking of secrets," he remarked with a grin, "while you're at it you can also tell me about your new boyfriend."

She gave him a startled look. "Where did you hear about that? I only told Victoria and Paul."

"Word gets around," he said. "It's the talk of the upper class, you know: prov-valley pilot Ito and that amazing Eridanian dreg, Stiletto. . . ." He chuckled. "Interesting surname, that. I never met anyone named after an assassin's weapon before. But outsystem colonists are strange folk." His voice tapered off and he looked at Andrea; the color had drained from her face. She gaped at her old friend. An assassin's weapon?

"I don't believe it," she said softly to herself. Then she took a deep, steadying breath. "Well, Linc, I'd better get going. I'll come visit you in a couple of days."

Stiletto: a narrow blade with a diamond-shaped cross section — easily hidden, or slipped between the ribs into the heart. A secret weapon, a silent one. Andrea looked it up in her dictionary as soon as she got back to the dorm.

And with the name Jason had chosen for his ship: *Blaze'a'Glory*. . . .

He did plan to do the Hammer in — and did not expect to get away alive.

She glanced around the room. Her three female classmates had gone to bed. Victoria, in the bed next to Andrea's, hugged her feather pillow to her chest, tangled in her covers with a bare foot protruding to the side. Andrea wanted to wake her up; she wished desperately that she could talk to someone.

I don't know if Jason plans to murder Trammerden, she reminded herself. *If only I were certain.*

She had better confront Jason again, right away. She sighed and stood. Before he did something incredibly stupid.

The corridor was dark; dim foot lights created shining pools on the acrylic floor. Jason set down his bag of tools, lifted a swathed Sssrei out and unwrapped it, and set it down on the floor. Then he slung the bag onto his back. The tools inside made a muffled clanking noise. Jason stilled the bag against his side.

"Keep watch, Sssrei."

The alien transmitted apprehension. "Proceed with caution."

Jason threw his companion a sardonic glance and crouched next to Tram's door.

It had taken several hours to break Tram's lock code and another hour and a half to steal a pair of stethophones and a laser scalpel from the med center. He would need high intensity heat to burn his way through the door of Tram's safe. He'd just have to hope he could burn through the titanium safe wall before the laser scalpel overheated and turned molten in his hand.

Sssrei rolled up behind him and extended its optic filaments over his shoulder as he slid the stethophones onto his head.

"If there *is* a safe," Sssrei remarked.

"Shut up. I'm trying to hear."

Jason listened. He adjusted the steth's muting controls on his right ear and turned up the volume; if Tram were awake he would eventually have to make a sound. The brush of cloth against cloth, even the whisper of a yawn — Jason would hear it.

He listened, unmoving, until his legs began to cramp. Not a sound, except perhaps the faintest of deep, measured breaths. Trammerden was asleep.

He swept the steth off his head, stuffed it into his bag, and pulled the magneto-key he had programmed that afternoon from his breast pocket. He slid the card into the slot by the door and held his breath.

The door dissolved in a watercolor glow. He released his breath, gave Sssrei a thumbs-up sign, and entered the room. The door resolved behind him.

The room was pitch black, except for a rectangle on the carpet of eerie, dim green light from the bedroom. Jason waited for his eyes to adjust, then walked lightly, on the balls of his feet, toward the bedroom door.

Tram lay propped up on pillows in bed, his head to the side and his mouth open. His bedside terminal was lit; he had fallen asleep while reading.

Jason was drawn into the room. He padded silently to the bed and looked down at his old enemy. It had only been three years. Three years — and Tram had aged. So much.

Jason studied Tram: lips thin and wide, turned up in the slight smile that Jason hated; eyes with round, heavy lids; a predator's nose; wide, pale forehead with temples laced with dark, serpentine veins. His hands rested on the covers, long and narrow, with curled, tapered fingers. A pilot's hands, quick and steady. Tram was a man now, a powerful and amoral man. Even in his sleep he emanated terrifying power.

He was the same, though. Time had not altered him. It had merely refined him, honed down the roughness, the unfinished edges of Trammerden's youth. Tram was elegant and deadly. A far more formidable enemy than he had been before.

Then Jason stared at his own hand in sudden fear, shaking himself free of the vertigo that had seized him. He had, unconsciously, reached out to touch Trammerden's ghost-green cheek.

Enemy-bond, Sssrei had called it: the link between two like Shenn, locked in mortal combat. Like telepathy, only more primal, more deadly. The bond would last — consuming their thoughts, gnawing at their souls, drawing them into conflict again and again — till one of them died.

Jason thrust the comparison away. I'm not a Shenn. I'm not really even a telepath. And I'm nothing like Tram.

He turned and went into the front room.

Andrea paused at the entrance to Jason's dorm. His senior dormmates were bound to be asleep at this hour; it was well past curfew, and the miniature cleaning robots were the only things moving in the corridors. Them and me, she thought.

Jason was probably sound asleep, too. She had a brief vision of herself waking him up to demand what his intentions toward Trammerden were, and him blinking sleepily at her, asking in tones saturated with polite sarcasm if her questions couldn't wait until a more reasonable hour. . . .

With a growl of frustration, she opened the door. It was his fault she wasn't in bed, resting up for her written finals. She wouldn't be able to sleep until she talked to him. And he'd embroiled her in this mess on the eve of her graduation. As if she didn't have enough to worry about.

Her ire carried her into the room and to the edge of his bed. Enough light was cast by the various time logs and terminals for her to see that his bed was empty.

The implications dawned on her slowly. Then came the horror. She was too late! With a gasp, she sprinted out of the room and raced down the hall.

She had to stop him.

Jason took out his needle light, knelt, and searched the floor with his fingers and eyes. The most likely location for the safe was under the carpeting, behind the desk. His heartrate leapt — there was a seam!

Carefully he peeled back the layers of cloth and foam rubber. A circle of gleaming silver: the safe. Jason took out the laser scalpel.

He burned around the perimeter of the circle using quick bursts of energy. The metal of the safe door hissed and sputtered loudly, while smoke stung his eyes and nostrils. He squinted against the blue brilliance and cast several glances toward the bedroom. Several times he paused to listen, heart pounding. But Trammerden did not awaken. Finally, Jason finished and with wedges and tongs pried the safe's lid off.

He pulled the data lattices and faxes out, then glanced over them. A newsfax dated August 29, 2106. The day Jason had undergone his harvest.

Page one was titled

A PERMANENT PEACE?
Delegates Congregate on Ceres
to Discuss Terms of Treaty

Captioned, color holos were splashed across the page, and several columns of print discussed the upcoming conference, scheduled for September 11. Three days from tomorrow. This peace conference was major news. Why hadn't he heard about it?

It was not the only newsfax for August 29, though. As he flipped through the pages he found another newsfax dated that same day. It was identical to the first, with only one difference: news of the conference on Ceres was missing. The second newsfax started on page two, with news of crop failure in Mexico and a story about the start-up of a new tolyernet amplifier between Sol and Proxima Centauri. In the upper right hand corner of this fax, new page numbers had been pasted over the originals. This was the fax Jason remembered reading.

There were more altered newsfaxes, spanning the last couple of weeks. Tram had removed all mention of the upcoming conference from the faxes before they were distributed among the students and staff. Jason frowned. Why? What difference did it make to Trammerden whether anyone knew about the conference?

Jason stuffed the faxes into his bag and looked through the remaining faxsheets. And he began to understand.

There was a faxcomm addressed to Tram, dated September 1. The note was unsigned, but the originating city, laser-traced across the top, was Calais-deux — the La Grange city that housed the Earth Aggregate Board of Directors.

The note was brief and decidedly cold: "This had better settle matters between us." Following was a string of numbers.

They were coordinates and window calcs for two sets of trajectories: one set from a source about the orbit of Jupiter and the other from about the orbit of Earth. The two sets of coordinates would converge at a location on the asteroid belt on September 10.

There were several pages of ballistic calculations and holocharts based on the coordinates from the note, and other calculations labeled in block letters: "INTERCEPT TRAJECTORIES." One set of intercept calculations had a note in the margin, *"Optimum — ? ?"* underscored with heavy black lines, with arrows and exclamation marks around it.

Trammerden intended to intercept the peace delegates before they reached Ceres.

It fit. If the delegation ships were destroyed, war would erupt. The power vacuum created would beg for someone to step in and take control.

"Sssrei — ?"

"Here, Jason," the alien replied, "you are excited."

"I've got my proof," he said and stood. He picked up the bag and the scalpel. How Tram planned to intercept the delegates did not matter. Jason had enough to finish him for good and all. He replaced the safe and laid the carpet over it.

Then panic — Sssrei's panic — slammed into his mind.

"Jason — *someone comes*!"

Someone was at the door! Jason looked around — no place to hide. He dashed for the door as the light came on, and Trammerden came into the room.

Trammerden blinked, seeing Jason. Several emotions ran across his face, chiefly mild surprise, then annoyance. And that unnerving presence. Jason's mind switched from stunned paralysis to computer mode — thinking, thinking. He still had his laser scalpel in hand. He slid the scalpel into his sleeve.

The door chimed again. Jason stepped forward.

"Why don't we see who's at the door?" he said. Trammerden grasped his wrist in a grip so hard it ground the bones together.

"I think not," the man said coolly. "Not until you explain what you're doing in my room, young man. What is your name?"

Jason met his gaze and held it. He smiled a hard smile into Trammerden's eyes. "Don't you recognize me, Tram?"

Within the space of a second, the expression on Trammerden's face changed from arrogant self-possession, through confusion, to fearful suspicion, to realization and shock. He went ghastly white.

"You." He spat the word.

"Me." Jason wrenched his arm free. The door chimed again, insistently; Trammerden jumped slightly. Jason pulled out his laser scalpel and leveled it at Trammerden. "Open the door, Tram. I have some things they might be interested to see."

Trammerden's glance flickered to Jason's weapon; he studied Jason through heavy-lidded eyes. Jason began to tremble. He clenched his teeth, forced the tremors down.

"Open the door," he repeated harshly.

"It's Andrea, Jason. She is leaving, at a run. Shoot him, or he will kill you!" Sssrei's thought was desperate.

A slow smile curled Trammerden's lips. "Not just yet," he said.

He rebelted his wine-colored dressing gown with his elegant hands, crossed to the gel couch, and sat down.

"Why don't you sit down and relax, Jason? You don't look too well."

Jason's teeth were chattering. His throat had spasmed shut. Kill him, he told himself. His body betrayed him; he stood motionless.

Sudden rage gave him speech, of a sort. He forced the words out through locked teeth. "Get up." Pause. "Or I will kk." Long pause. "Kill you."

Trammerden affected amused surprise. He laughed. "Come now. We both know you'll do no such thing. Why don't you put your toy away and have a seat? It's been such a long time since I've seen you." He patted the cushion. "No need to be so nervous, Jason. I'm an old friend. And I'm sure you have a lot to tell me. For instance, how is it you're back in Sol so soon? I hadn't planned on your reappearance for at least another fifteen years."

Jason shook himself violently, trying to activate the scalpel. His hand had frozen on the grip. He stared at the laser and looked up in dull horror. Trammerden shook his head with a doleful sigh, and stood.

"I was hoping for more of a challenge," Trammerden said, as he plucked the scalpel from Jason's nerveless fingers, and dropped it on the carpet. "You're a real disappointment, Jason." He put his hand into his dressing gown pocket.

Jason's vision was going; his knees buckled and the world turned on its end. Fire. Consuming the last of his oxygen. His ears were ringing, there were shouts in his head, I'm dying help me Jason are you all right pain I'm burning I'm suffocating open the door let me die or we'll break it down jason jason it's me sssrei I hurt you're dreaming chimes crushing pain can't breathe soundless concussions the smell of charring flesh metal and vacuum and fire icy cold I'm freezing I'm burning jasonJASON he killed me tram I'll get you get you killed me die let me die letmedieLETMEDIE —

And then the nightmare faded into oblivion.

Andrea stood at the door, numbed by shock. Jason lay on the carpet, his hands clutched over his ears and his face a mask of agony and terror. Senior Admin Trammerden stood over him, a sonic palmgun in his hand. The older man had an unreadable expression on his face as he looked down at Jason.

The two security people pushed past Andrea.

"He broke in and tried to kill me," Trammerden told the chief of security. His voice was flat and emotionless. He had not taken his eyes off Jason. Andrea wondered if he were in shock.

"Lock him up," Trammerden said. "I'll want to question him later."

They picked Jason up under the arms and carried him away.

Andrea turned with them, but the Hammer's voice called her back. She turned around. A thrill of fear coursed through her at the lack of emotion in his eyes.

"Colleague Ito. I take it you were the one at the door earlier."

She nodded, staring at him, unwilling to speak, or even to think. The older man came forward and laid a hand on her shoulder. She flinched.

"You saved my life," he said. "If you hadn't rung my doorchime, I'd be dead. My thanks."

She swallowed, straightened. "You're welcome," she said. It sounded inane. "May I go now, sir? I have finals in four hours and I haven't slept. . . ."

He pinned her with a look. "Of course, Colleague. But how did you know my life was in danger?"

"I . . ." Andrea took a calming breath. She had done her duty; she had saved the Senior Administrator's life. She owed the man no more than that.

Rogue-friend, she thought. Everyone knows

about Jason and me. But maybe, since I stopped him. . . .

She did not finish the thought. She was relieved that it had been she who stopped him and ashamed of her relief.

"I saw him enter your room, sir. I didn't know he was breaking in, but I thought it was strange that a dreg would be coming to your quarters so late, so I decided to come back and check. And when you didn't answer your door. . . ."

He studied her for a long, uncomfortable moment, then nodded. "You may go."

Through the resolving door she watched him pick up the bag that had fallen from Jason's shoulder, remove some faxes from it, and study them. His expression was surprised, then thoughtful. Clinical.

She headed down the hall, then spun and went into fight stance. She had heard something, a soft clatter.

Jason's Eridani pet, or friend, was rolling toward her on its spikes. It stopped a short distance from her feet and extended its glass fibers toward her.

"Go away," she told it. "Your friend just tried to murder someone and he's under arrest."

She turned and kept walking. It followed. She turned again. "Look, you. I know you understand English. Go away." She kicked at it halfheartedly. It backed just outside her range and sat motionless, its weird stalks riveted on her. She groaned.

"Just go on, okay? I feel rotten. I want to get some sleep. Why are you following me? Why didn't you follow Jason?"

It made no indication of having understood a word she'd said. With a sigh of frustration, she picked up the alien — what did Jason call it? a Shenn? and tucked it under her arm the way she had seen him carry it.

Back in the dorm, she set the alien in her pile of dirty laundry by the bed, turned off her light, then undressed and slid under the covers.

The alien's stalks moved around, tips glowing like a hundred eyes in the dark. They moved toward her and touched her cheek. She brushed the filaments away. The creature gave her the creeps.

She closed her eyes, tried to relax, counted to ten thousand, recited to herself the names of the moons of all the planets. It was no use. Sleep escaped her.

Chapter 14

Andrea opened her eyes. It seemed as if she had just closed them. Victoria was shaking her gently. "Come on, Andy — get up."

Andrea rolled over with a moan. "What time is it?"

"After seven. Tests start in twenty minutes." Victoria tugged at the covers. "Get out of bed, Ito."

"I'm up," she said and swung her legs over the side, picked up her terrycloth robe, and slid it on. She scratched her head and yawned. "Can't believe I slept so late." Then she saw the alien by the bed and remembered. Jason.

The creature had rolled over to Victoria's desk and sat at the base of the chair with its slender stalks pointed at the terminal. Its stalks swayed toward Andrea, then back to the terminal. Victoria was looking at the creature also.

"It was there when I got up this morning. I can't get it to move. I was about to call Housekeeping to pick it up. Can't figure how it got in here."

"You don't have to call Housekeeping. I

brought it in." Andrea pushed herself to her feet. "I'm taking care of it for a while."

Victoria seemed surprised. "For your friend Jason?"

Andrea nodded, sighed. "He was arrested last night. He tried to kill the Hammer."

"What?" Anya burst out with an exclamation of disbelief. Even Nöel, a skinny girl from the notorious tunnelwalks of the east coast US — who never reacted to anything — turned and stared.

"What happened?" Anya asked.

Andrea pulled a clean uniform from her wardrobe and slipped it on. Her stomach was in knots. Fine way to start finals. "I'll tell you guys after the tests," she said.

She ignored the others' murmurs and went into the bathroom to brush her hair and wash up.

Victoria came to the door behind her. "Are you okay, Andy?"

Andrea dried her face with a towel and turned.

"Yeah. Just a little shocked, I guess."

Victoria folded her arms. She looked as though she did not know what to say. "No one'll blame you, Andy."

Andrea shook her head. "It's late. Let's talk later."

Victoria's eyes grew hard.

"Slag it, Ito, why are you always so distrustful? Your boyfriend tries to kill the Senior Administrator — and you don't want to talk about it." She broke off, then said coldly,

"You're close to roguing on our friendship, Colleague, and I'm getting a little tired of it."

Andrea stared at her, numb.

Victoria's expression turned to chagrin. She pinched the lines from her brow with a sigh.

"I'm sorry," she said. "I'm . . . just tense, I guess."

"Forget it," Andrea replied. But the accusation had cut deep.

"Guys, come look!" Anya called. "It's got wings!"

Andrea followed Victoria back into the room. The little alien had unfolded membranes of shimmering glass from vertical slits on its sides, behind its optical fibers. It had rolled the membranes into tubes and was extending them upward toward the desktop. The girls gathered around to watch.

"What's it doing?" Victoria asked. Andrea tossed the towel onto her bed and joined the others.

The keyboard rested on the edge of the desk. The tips of the creature's membranes found the keyboard and moved up to the keys. It could just barely reach the lower two rows.

Andrea moved closer. It had struck several keys. The screen displayed:

HL JASN ANDA HL M FND JASN

Then the creature furled its membranes. Slivers of glass were left behind on the keys.

Anya laughed uneasily. "Weird."

Victoria touched Andrea's arm. "Come on, we're going to be late."

Andrea stared at the screen, then at the

creature. It was trying to communicate with her. Something about Jason.

The others were waiting at the door. She pointed a finger at the creature and enunciated clearly, "Wait right here. I'll be back in eight hours. You understand? Stay right here."

Then she ran to catch up with the others.

Awareness returned slowly. Jason lay flat on his back on a hard, lumpy surface which seemed to be rocking back and forth. He opened his eyes to harsh, fluorescent light. His head hurt. He sat up. Waves of nausea assaulted him. He sat still until they passed, then looked around.

He was in the isolation cell in Security. There was a toilet, a sink, and a cot. He stood — and nearly fell over. Trammerden had used sonics on him.

Jason groped for the edge of the cot and sat down. Well, it could be worse. He could be dead.

How long had he been out, anyhow? Was it the tenth yet? Jason fought down a surge of anxiety. No sense in stripping his wires; he had probably only been unconscious a day — or less. Eventually he would have contact with someone. For now he would just have to wait.

Through the clear field of the door a security automaton, a floating cylinder with four long mechanical arms about its circumference, monitored him. There were cam-I's in the corners of the room.

"How about something to eat?" he said to the room at large. There was no response, but he had not really expected one.

Eventually he was able to come to his feet without losing his balance. He walked to the door and touched the field. Its texture was like cold metal charged with a low voltage current — shivers of pale lightning spread from where his fingers had touched it, across the surface of the field. The automaton moved closer. Jason eyed the machine and then sat back down on his cot. His head throbbed.

He concentrated.

"Sssrei?" He opened his mind, reached out. No greeting answered him, not even a hint of the Shenn's presence. Nothing better to do, Jason thought ruefully, and kept trying.

Andrea stood outside Security, fuming. The entire section was closed off — restricted to all human personnel, the computer had just informed her in its polite contralto voice, except on the direct orders of Senior Administrator Trammerden.

"What do you mean, off limits? I'm Andrea Ito. Provisional valedictorian of the entire senior class. I'm the one responsible for the dreg's arrest!" She glared at the console by the door.

"Security cells are currently closed to human personnel," it replied in exactly the same tone as before. "You must obtain approval from Senior Administrator Trammerden before you may speak to the prisoner.

She slammed her hand against the wall and then stalked off down the corridor. She ran into a group of her classmates, but did not acknowledge their greetings.

I didn't do the wrong thing, she thought. I did what I had to. Jason was in the wrong; he stole supplies from the med center and broke into the Senior Administrator's quarters. He might have killed him. I couldn't let that happen.

She knew she had done well on the tests; she had known the material inside and out and had prepared well. Three more exams tomorrow, in Applied Xenogeology, Phys Ed and Advanced Tectogenetics Theory. After that she'd be done with everything but final graduation exercises — which, rumor had it, would be different, even more difficult than usual, this year. Jason MacLeod was not her problem any more.

If only I had gotten to him earlier. I might have talked him out of it.

And what to do about the alien? Send it back to 40 Eridani II? Andrea did not have that kind of money. And she did not have a clue how to care for it — or even how to communicate with it, really. It seemed to be able to use a keyboard, after a fashion, but its wings were not made to use a human keyboard; communication would be excruciatingly slow.

Well, at least it can tell me what it needs, she thought.

She took a shuttle across Collegium to the dorm section. When she got to her own dorm, Victoria was at her desk, studying. The little alien was nowhere to be seen.

"Where did it go?"

Victoria looked up. "When I opened the door it rolled out into the hall. It must have been waiting for someone to open the door. Is that a problem?"

Andrea frowned, uneasy. "I don't know. It seems terribly fragile. And it might spray someone." She sat down on her bed. "Well, it'll probably turn up eventually. I'm going to take a nap. Could you wake me up in a couple of hours?"

"Hmmm?" Victoria had returned to her console; she seemed distracted. "Sure."

Andrea curled up on her bed. She had not expected success, but she went to sleep almost immediately.

The day, and the night, passed slowly for Jason. He spent most of his time trying to contact Sssrei, with no luck. The security robot brought him a couple of meals, which he ate without tasting.

There was a moment when he almost felt Sssrei was near . . . but there was no answer to his call. Doggedly, he kept on.

The second day of tests came. The written tests were relatively easy; consequently Andrea's mind wandered. She aced her Applied Xenogeology exam. But she did not do as well as she should have in Tectogenetics Theory.

The Phys Ed test was in a mock-up of a real interstellar cruiser and was recreated from an incident that had really happened several years before, out beyond Pluto. Andrea,

Weasel, and ten other seniors from the different disciplines were crew members.

Seconds into the test, their shields failed, and they slammed into a cloud of hydrogen at 60% of the speed of light. Before there was time to evaluate and initiate repairs, an "engineer" turned rogue and detonated several nanograms of fuel. Andrea and the bridge crew scrambled for the pressure suit lockers before the concussions had entirely ceased. They would have to find and repair the breaches in the hull, then jury-rig a setup to send an emergency signal to the scientific outpost on Pluto.

It was too important; she had to pass. Andrea put aside thoughts of Jason and what had happened and focused on staying "alive" and passing the test.

There were several close calls and she lost a crewmember to strip-wired passengers, but she and the team passed. She found out that their scores were the highest of the entire senior class.

Victoria and Paul invited her to go with them to the rec center, where a movie was being aired. She went, but hardly paid attention. She kept thinking about Jason. Somehow the most desperate of all the simulated emergencies she had been subjected to seemed pale, a series of flimsy parodies.

Most of her classmates assumed she was tense about tomorrow's exercises. Only Victoria and Paul knew differently, but they said nothing, merely offered her silent companionship.

Very early the next morning, September 10, Andrea woke to a call on the comm. She stumbled out of bed and answered it; the physician who had taken care of Jason and the two seniors a couple of weeks before greeted her.

"Another student has been burned by the alien," the physician informed her. "I realize you're not duty officer today, but it was my understanding that you have a personal interest in the situation now, so I wanted to let you know...."

Andrea rubbed her face with a sigh. "What happened? How badly is the student hurt?"

"She has a couple of chemical burns."

The girl came onto the screen beside the physician. She was a senior whom Andrea knew slightly.

"I asked Dr. Talies to call you, Colleague. They said you were taking care of the creature now ... it was outside a door when I came out of my class yesterday afternoon, and I kicked it accidentally. My foot started itching in the middle of the night so I came to have it checked."

Andrea asked her for the location, then thanked her and signed off.

She went to the psychology classrooms and checked inside the room the girl had mentioned. She found the creature hiding under the teacher's desk. She knelt down; several of its fibers had broken off. When she reached for it, it rolled away. She noticed that a patch of its spherical body had also crumbled away. White powder and a small puddle of chemicals had formed under the alien. Ammonia stung her nostrils. She choked and wiped her nose and eyes.

"You're hurting, aren't you?" she said. Its fibers watched her silently. She removed her flight jacket, wrapped the little creature in it, and picked it up. Her hand brushed the injured area; it was coated with a sticky solid and had a thin, slick film of liquid over it. She wiped her hand on her jacket. "You're looking for Jason. I know. I wish you'd waited for me instead of rolling off on your own. Come on." She tucked it under her arm and headed out the door. "I only hope you have better luck getting through to him than I did."

Jason sat crosslegged on his cot. He had not moved nor slept for hours; his mind was still reaching out for Sssrei. His legs were stiff and his back hurt. He ignored the discomfort.

Jason knew patience; time had been his enemy before. But he had to reach Sssrei quickly. Had to. He had figured out how Trammerden planned to do in the peace delegates.

Then, gradually, he realized that he had a sense of Sssrei's presence. He smoothed the muscles of his face; cam-I's were watching. The Shenn's mental presence grew stronger.

"Sssrei, where are you? You're in pain. . . ."

"Jason! You're alive." Waves of relief emanated from the Shenn, washing out the pain he sensed radiating from it. "I feared you were dead."

"I'm all right, for the time being. I suspect

Tram's too busy to bother with me, at the moment. What day is it, do you know? How much time has passed since we broke into Tram's quarters?"

Sssrei transmitted the length of time: two days and a few hours.

So it was early morning on the tenth.

"Where are you now?"

Sssrei hesitated. "The Andrea-human is carrying me. I think she's trying to take me to you." There was another pause. "We have stopped outside a door and she is setting me down. What shall I do, Jason? I do not know how to free you."

Jason shook his head. "Don't worry about freeing me, friend. You have to find some way to get through to Andrea. I figured out how Trammerden plans to destroy the delegates' ships. He's going to use the graduation exercises. The senior pilots are the only fleet he controls, and the timing is too convenient to be coincidental."

Jason sat forward and gripped the edge of the cot. "Tell Andrea, Sssrei. She's our only chance."

Sssrei's thoughts were doubtful. "She does not trust us. She will not believe me."

"You have to convince her, Sssrei. It's our only chance. Hurry. We only have a couple of hours."

He repeated it, quelling a wave of panicked frustration. "Hurry."

The alien sat without moving, outside the

door to Security. Andrea stood over it and watched for a few minutes, then propped herself against the wall. She had no idea whether it was talking to Jason, or what it would do afterwards.

She looked at her chronometer. Six-fifty-eight. She still had to change and report to the launch bay by seven-thirty. She eyed the creature. Its filaments were staring at the door.

Should she leave it here or take it with her?

She squatted next to it; a number of fibers swayed to look at her.

"I have to leave." She hesitated. "I wish I knew whether you could understand me. Shall I take you with me? I can bring you back after exercises."

No response. She stood up, took a couple of steps, then turned and waited.

The creature seemed to understand; it rolled after her.

"All right, then," she said, and picked it up.

The other girls in the dorm were hurriedly getting ready. Victoria spun on Andrea.

"Where have you been? The Hammer has summoned us fifteen minutes early."

Andrea set the alien down on the bed and whipped a clean flight suit out of the wardrobe. Fear surged in her. This was it.

The alien was rolling for the edge of the bed. She caught it before it fell off.

"I don't have time for games," she snapped at it, pulling on her soft cotton shirt. She velled the front and sleeves.

Victoria snatched up her bag. The other two girls, with rushed good-byes, dashed out the door.

"Shall I wait?"

Andrea waved Victoria on and pulled on her pants. "Go. I'll be right behind you."

She pulled her hair back to braid it; her fingers were trembling.

The alien almost rolled off the bed again. It was staring at her desk computer.

"Stop it!" Andrea caught the alien again and set it on the desk. Her hair would not cooperate. She was going to be late.

She could not find her flight cap. She dug through her bag, then dug through the pile of clothes by the bed. The alien was typing on the computer keyboard.

There it was — at the bottom of the pile. She snatched up the shiklon cap and jammed it into her flight bag.

The alien had typed a message.

GIV ME SOX

She paused, frowning at the alien. SOX. Socks? Then she looked at its membranes, which were shattering on the keys.

She dug a pair of socks out of the pile and slid them, quickly and carefully, over the creature's membranes. She grabbed her bag.

"Type to your heart's content," she said. "I'll read it when I get back."

The alien began, laboriously, to tap at the keys.

She ran out the door.

Chapter 15

Jason paced the enclosure with the restlessness of a caged cat. Almost three hours had passed since he had spoken to Sssrei.

Too soon to have word, yet. If Sssrei had found a way to contact Andrea, and if Andrea had believed it, and if she could persuade her classmates, Tram's plan would have failed by now. But Jason would not know until they came to release him, or to kill him.

Andrea was in danger. He had put her squarely opposed to Trammerden — if Sssrei had gotten through. And there was not a thing he could do to help her, or Sssrei, or even himself. He sat on the edge of the cot, running his hands through his hair. I shouldn't have involved you, Andrea.

Sssrei's presence broke into his thoughts. It was outside in the corridor. He sprang up.

"You're back," he said. "Tell me."

"I failed, Jason." Waves of remorse and pain poured from the alien's mind. "I was not quick enough. They are on their way."

Jason did not move for a long moment. Then

he sat down, carefully, like an old man. "Well, you gave it your best," he said. His voice came from a long way away. A slow rage began to burn in him; he made a fist of his shaking hand and slammed the fist into the wall. The pain did not kill the anger; he leapt to his feet and threw himself against the field door.

"Cease or you will injure yourself," the security robot said. He ignored it.

Smack. Smack. His body screamed outrage. Smack. Pain exploded in his right arm. He crouched, panting, and blinked through sweat and tears. The pain was vicious.

His rage spent itself. The automaton returned to its console. Jason collapsed on the cot and sobbed. Gradually, the pain faded.

Think, MacLeod. Think. There has to be a way. He got up, splashed icy water on his face, and then sat back down. An idea was teasing the back of his mind. Something he had done once. . . .

"Sssrei? Are you still there?"

The alien's thought was tentative, nervous. "I am still here. Do you have a plan?"

"No. I don't know." He thought for a moment. "I'm trying to recall the trajectories. Tram's calcs projected intercept at eleven-two. It's past ten now. I wish I knew exactly what time it is."

He thought for a few moments longer. Then he sprang to his feet and began to pace. "If only you could use a computer. . . ."

"I can," Sssrei said. "In a way."

It projected a picture of itself with sock-swathed membranes, typing at the keyboard. There was a tinge of growing hope in its thoughts. "If you tell me what to do. . . ."

Jason shook his head. "It'll be too difficult. You'd have to know how to do it. Maybe I could do it, but I can't get to a computer console. Could you pick the skill out of my head?"

"There isn't time." Sssrei was regretful. "It would take a long time to trace all the necessary knowledge lines to their sources. But there is another way. Join me in my mind."

Jason shook his head. "I can't."

"You can." Sssrei overrode his protests, patient. "I'll help you. It is not so difficult. See through my eyes, Jason. What am I looking at?"

"I can't." Jason threw himself onto the pillow and stared at the ceiling. He was suddenly terrified. He had had glimpses of Sssrei's mind. The power, the strangeness. It might drive him mad.

"I am no monster." Sssrei seemed frustrated. "I was not driven mad; neither will you be. It will seem perfectly natural. You must try."

It was hopeless. With a grunt of irritation, he said, "All right."

Jason shut his eyes and tried to see what Sssrei was seeing. Nothing happened. "There. You see?"

"You weren't trying. You must relax." At Jason's stubborn silence, it added bluntly, "Just how much do you want to stop Trammerden?"

Jason was silent. Then he nodded with a sigh. "You're right, as usual."

He closed his eyes and relaxed. Sssrei was there with him, very near. He pictured Sssrei standing next to him, in a human body — his body. His vision changed — he was seeing all directions at once. Everything was redder.

Shenn awareness saturated his thoughts. His mind was incredibly powerful: He knew how to blast into another's mind and destroy it. And he saw the restraints that kept that power dormant unless Sssrei's life was gravely threatened. He remembered growing up in heated caves, soaking in boiling liquid, and drinking sunlight. He remembered the time when the Shenn were one with their symbiotic companions, the Aabssa; he tumbled across a savannah of Shenndri at dizzying speeds, captured in a high wind.

"Not so bad, is it?" Sssrei sounded amused. Its thoughts were very close, warm, and comforting.

"There are memories you're shielding from me," Jason said.

"One thing at a time," Sssrei said. It allowed Jason control of its optic filaments, and he looked down at himself. Sssrei's body looked much larger than he remembered — and he was seeing it from all angles at once. His — Sssrei's — body was smooth and dark; it could not see the faint, warm glow of its own interior as Jason could. Their sight must be shifted into the ultraviolet, he thought.

His vision was not so distinct, but it had infinitely more depth. The doors lining the corridor were brilliant blue-white, not deep purple. When he shifted his sight, objects left ghost trails. Dark, fuzzy material blanketed his photo-receptive membranes, which hung from his sides. Socks. Looking about made him feel, inexplicably, as if he needed to sneeze.

He was vaguely aware of discomfort, punctuated by needles of pain. Sssrei was injured.

"Not seriously," it said. "I'll recover."

"It's so silent."

"Among my people," Sssrei said, "your mind would be filled with sound and music. But I have come to value this silence. Come."

Jason felt the spikes along his spherical body extrude and retract. The hall turned over; it proceeded and receded before and behind him.

Long legs, a human's, strode past, stopped, and turned as Sssrei moved. Jason listened to Sssrei's thoughts; it was counting doorways — retracing its path. It remembered a console that was close enough to the floor for it to reach the controls.

Jason found the location in Sssrei's mind. A housekeeping station, where the cleaning robots plugged in to receive their instructions. "Good, Sssrei. Very good."

The console approached, righting itself as Sssrei came to a halt. Jason felt Sssrei stepping back, handing the controls over to him.

"It's all yours," Sssrei said.

Jason lifted his membranes tentatively. They came up, stiff stumps. This was not going to be easy. Awkwardly, he logged in on the computer keyboard and entered his user number and password. Print ran across the screen; he tried to focus on it. The words were dim, and the wrong color.

"You need specs, Sssrei," he thought. Sssrei transmitted amusement. The computer had reached the GO, level. He typed in &CLOCK and the computer displayed the time. It was ten-nineteen. He had half an hour.

Just in case Tram was not as thorough as Jason feared, he tried to get into the comm software.

GO, &RUN TELECAST

ERROR ON USERCODE ⟨⟨JM@626L4⟩⟩. INSUFFICIENT ACCESS RIGHTS.

GO, —

Jason eyed the screen. He was not surprised. Tram would have to be an idiot not to shut down radio communications before trying a crime like this. Couldn't have the comm personnel hear the delegates' cries for help when the senior class opened fire on them.

It was as bad as he had feared. The only lines open were the automatic ones, and almost all of those would be impossible to break into quickly.

But there was one line he knew about that he had broken into before: the signals that came from Collegium computers to position the school's network of force field satellites. Drastic changes were not allowed by the computer. But small manual corrections were made all the time. Jason had repositioned shield network satellites a number of times when he was a junior and senior.

Even the autocomm lines would be monitored

by Tram's security software. But they had to remain open, or Collegium's defense would be hampered. He should be able to get a short burst of data out before his avenue was blocked. It would have to be brief, and broadcast radially, over a ten degree span, toward Ceres.

With agonizing slowness, he programmed the message with his socked stumps. He named the file HELP. Then he went back to the GO, mode and checked the time. He had eight minutes. He was out of time. If this didn't work, nothing would.

He entered &RUN CHGFLD. The computer came back and asked for the satellite whose position was to be altered. He requested a list of their ID numbers and positions, and chose three satellites that lay in the direction of Ceres.

The computer requested the new data. Here goes, Jason thought. He gave the computer an invisible command — ΛUΛO, which would force the satellites to transmit the data, rather than try to process them — and typed in ACCEPT HELP. Then he deleted the file and logged out.

"Let's get you out of here, Sssrei. Before they come looking for us."

Andrea had made a surprising discovery. The main feature of a "real" mission, so far, was turning out to be that it was incredibly dull.

The radio silence Trammerden had insisted upon was the problem; she had not heard the voices of her team since they had left Collegium almost three and a half hours before. She was alone. The only sounds were the throaty hum of her engines and an occasional soft click as her craft's sensory mechanisms completed a scan of empty space, looking for the enemy ship, the fox. But there was no sign of the fox, or its convoy. She wondered how Victoria and her team were doing.

The fox would not be alone; Trammerden had said that it would be part of a convoy — four drones would be protecting it. The drones would be firing real weapons and would be programmed for surprise tactics. Be prepared, he had said. Your lives will depend on your performance.

Jason had nearly died during his grad exercises. And that had been a normal fox-chase. Jason.

This mission was giving Andrea entirely too much time to think. She thought about the time he had kissed her. About what he had told her of 40 Eridani II, the dwarf suns they called the Monkey and the Weasel, and the way he had smiled; the only real smile she had ever seen on his face. And about how he had asked her to trust him.

So little time; they had been given so little time. And now he was chilling it in a security cell — she would probably never see him again. He would be tried for murder and sentenced to one of the prison mines.

On second thought, she probably would see him again, at his trial. Her testimony would be called for. She was directly responsible for Jason's capture. Trammerden had said so, himself.

The most frightening part was the tiny sliver of uncertainty in the corner of her mind. He might not have been there to kill Trammerden. Perhaps the Senior Admin had been mistaken. . . .

But she remembered the look on his face when he had fought the sparring robot, and his screams when he had twitched out, during the fizz test. He had wanted Trammerden to hurt the way he had hurt. He wanted Tram dead. There was no other reason he would break into his quarters.

Andrea thrust the uncertainty away with a violent shake of her head. What had happened could not be helped. She had saved a man's life.

The Senior Administrator had been at his charismatic best before the launch. Andrea and her teammates had stood in a neat row before the fighter craft while Trammerden gave them a speech.

He had spoken of the war. He had said that the pilots' exercise this year would mirror a real war mission, rather than a fox-chase.

"Hard times require hard choices," he had said. And, "To give the exercise more of a semblance of reality, the drones will be programmed to fight back. They've been programmed with state-of-the-art software, so don't underestimate them. As in a real battle situation, disregard all attempts by the enemy to communicate."

He had divided the pilots into two groups, to give everyone a chance to make a showing, and issued them their flight orders. Andrea glanced at hers.

She would be team leader. The trajectories were all precalculated. They were to maintain radio silence until the convoy was engaged. They would be judged not on their individual performances, but on their team performance.

Victoria would lead the other team; Paul was with her.

Trammerden had then pulled Andrea aside. "Colleague Ito, Commander Turin has suggested that you might be interested in staying on at Collegium in a professional capacity."

Andrea gasped. An amused smile appeared on the Senior Admin's face. She said carefully, "Why, yes, I would, sir. I was going to submit my application after exercises."

The older man had regarded her closely, his eyes glittering. "I'll be frank, Colleague. You show great promise as a pilot — and I want to show my gratitude for your assistance the other night. If you perform well in exercises, you will have a place with us."

Andrea had felt blood rush to her face. She thanked the Senior Administrator profusely and then joined her teammates at their ships, sending silent thanks to Linc. Her mind was reeling with the impact of Trammerden's offer. If I pull this off, I'm in!

Andrea shook off her reverie. Rendezvous with the convoy would occur in six minutes. She activated her long-range tracker. Nothing yet. She wondered if Jason had been scared. She sure was.

Then the convoy appeared, a fuzz of amber on the farthest edge of her tracker. She started on an intercept course; her teammates followed suit. Her heart was racing.

It's just an exercise, she thought. They'll handicap the wolves; it'd be irrational to wipe out your seniors in a grad exercise. She took a deep breath and cut off the fox's signals.

Then she glanced at her panel. Her comm light had lit up suddenly. A message from Collegium. Odd — the Hammer had said Collegium would maintain radio silence.

She switched the data console over.

MACLEOD2ITO ABORTABORT FOX=PEACE
DELEG@JI;/@%rRX #&:

Andrea stared at the message fragment, Jason, in a guarded security cell, had broken through the comm blackout. But he was in detention. There was no way he could have gotten a message out; this was a test from Trammerden.

No, that didn't make sense. The Senior Admin did not know she knew Jason's real last name.

FOX=PEACE DELEG. Fox equals peace delegates?

Her brain flashed to a string of memories. The faxes on Trammerden's desk that dealt with an offensive strike. Weasel's insistence that he had read an article about a peace conference on Ceres that no one else had read. The papers in Jason's bag, when he had broken into Trammerden's room, and the look on the Senior Admin's face as he had studied them.

She reached toward her comm console, then

drew her hand back. This was too nightmarish to be true. Jason's paranoia was infecting her. The Hammer would never send Collegiate cadets to wipe out a peace envoy. She looked again at the four escort ships. They were little more than splinters of light; her holo-tracker showed them altering course to meet her ships.

Microseconds were passing. Indecision would be lethal. She needed to make the right decision — swiftly.

It was actually a simple calculation: What were the choices, and what were the consequences of choosing wrongly?

Case one: The message was false. If she did not abort, she and her team would ace the exercises and graduate with great honors.

If she aborted, her career was ruined. She would have a smear across her record that would make her Collegium degree worthless. And not only that, she would have betrayed her classmates. She would deserve every iota of hostility and scorn she would be subjected to.

And for what? For nothing. For a crazy dreg she hardly knew, who had tried to kill Collegium's Senior Admin.

Case two: The message was true. If she did not abort and Jason had, against all reason, been right, she was at the very least an accomplice to murder. And more — she would be abetting an attempt to precipitate war.

The stakes were too high. She couldn't take the chance that Jason was rogue.

The escort ships had formed into a wedge; far behind them was the cigar shape of the fox.

Warning shots burst about her craft in a stunningly beautiful gold halo; Andrea's craft trembled slightly. Her teammates were beginning their scatter.

She slammed on the radio, traced onto her comrades, and sent them a tight-beam, scrambled broadcast.

"Hold your fire."

In the same instant, the voice of the fox's alarmed comm officer filled her ears.

". . . the Earth Aggregate Ship *Frontier*. Please identify yourselves, or we must assume hostile intent. Please identify yourselves."

The tension ebbed from her muscles; she sat back with a careful sigh. Her faint reflection in the cockpit window stared glassily back at her. She was drenched in sweat; her arms felt leaden and the muscles of her thighs ached.

I can't believe it, she thought, quite calmly. Jason was telling the truth.

Her teammates' confused voices acknowledged her broadcast. She inhaled and sat forward. It wasn't over yet. Andrea switched the comm over to wide-beam unscrambled transmission.

"*Frontier*, this is Andrea Ito of Collegium. We were out on grad exercises and scanned you on our trackers. What is your destination?"

Her earjack crackled. "We're the E.A. peace delegation to Ceres," the voice replied. "You had us pretty worried there for a minute. You're awfully far from Collegium runs, aren't you?"

"We lost our fox."

"Rotten luck," the comm officer said. His voice carried puzzlement.

His surprise might congeal into suspicion; Andrea added swiftly, "Well, since our fox is gone, may we offer you an escort to Ceres?"

There was a pause. The comm officer came back on. "We'd be delighted, Colleague."

Victoria and her team were too far away for a tight-beam voice signal — and the other delegate ship might intercept it and discover the blunder. Swiftly, Andrea programmed a scrambled data transmission on a Collegium wavelength for Victoria.

ITO TO JAMISON. URGENT. ABORT EXERCISE. FOX CONTAINS TMC PEACE DELEGATES. REPEAT, ABORT EXERCISE. ACKNOWLEDGE.

She set it to repeat several times and sat back, knuckles white on her couch arms.

Agonizing minutes later, her colleague responded. Letters moved across her screen:

ABORTED. WEASEL FLASHED BUT I SURE DON'T. HOPE YOU KNOW WHAT YOU'RE DOING. VJ.

Andrea sat back. Exercise aborted. For the first time in history, the system-renowned Collegium grad exercises didn't happen.

Andrea and her team fell in with the other fighter craft and settled in for a long trek to Ceres. Andrea thought long and hard.

There was no way this could be an accident. The Senior Admin had planned for them to wipe out two ships filled with peace delegates. He was everything Jason had said: an evil, self-serving man. He had tried to start a savage, cataclysmic war.

As Andrea thought about it, anger began to build in her. He had tried to use her, and the others, to bring about a war that would kill millions.

She had acted initially to protect her team, to recover Collegium's neutrality, but the Senior Admin was the one who had violated that neutrality. Not Andrea and her team. Jon Trammerden was clearly a dangerous man. He had to be stopped.

When they reached Ceres, Andrea would request an audience with the E.A. and Commonwealth reps. They should be most interested to hear what she had to say.

It was approximately four minutes after mission abort. Andrea's comm light came on again. Jason?

She switched on the comm.

TRAMMERDEN TO ITO.

She stared at the screen, abruptly dry-mouthed.

I KNOW YOU'RE RECEIVING THIS, AND I KNOW ABOUT THE MESSAGE MACLEOD SENT YOU. I'VE BEEN MONITORING THE ENGAGEMENT. YOUR LITTLE LIE TO THE DELEGATES WAS A WISE MOVE, COLLEAGUE. IF YOU CONTINUE TO ACT WISELY, MACLEOD & YOUR FRIEND TURIN WILL BE SAFE. OTHERWISE, OF COURSE, I HAVE NO REASON TO KEEP THEM ALIVE.

ACKNOWLEDGE.

She sat motionless, looking at the screen. Her hands were trembling again.

After a long pause, the screen read, DON'T FORCE ME TO ACT, COLLEAGUE. YOU HAVE FIVE

SECONDS TO RESPOND, OR I WILL GIVE THE ORDER
TO HAVE MACLEOD & TURIN EXECUTED. ACKNOWL-
EDGE.

"No." The word burst from her, a whispered
explosion of air. She could not let him kill Jason
and Linc.

Andrea tapped out a message and transmitted
it.

IF I PROMISE TO REMAIN QUIET, YOU'LL
GUARANTEE THEIR SAFETY?

MY WORD ON IT.

Andrea eyed Trammerden's reassurance,
chewing her nail. It was their only chance. She
typed in an acknowledgement. THEN I'LL
COOPERATE.

After an agonizing delay, a signal came back
in. VERY GOOD, COLLEAGUE. ANOTHER WISE
CHOICE; I'M SURE CMDR TURIN & YOUR FRIEND
MACLEOD WILL BE GRATEFUL. NOW MAKE YOUR
APOLOGIES TO THE FOX AND RETURN TO
COLLEGIUM AT TOP SPEED.

Andrea beamed a quick message to *Frontier*
and ordered her team to fall in behind her.

Once they had put the delegates far behind
them, Thomas's voice came onto the comm. His
voice sounded strange.

"Hey, Ito, give us a transmit! I'm a little
tangled about all this."

"Later, Colleague," she said softly, and dis-
engaged her radio. She removed her throat
mike, leaned her head against the head rest, and
closed her eyes. She wanted desperately to cry,
but tears would not come.

Chapter 16

It had the texture, the inevitability of a dream. She shut down her ship's drive as the little craft slipped into the dock funnel; violet petals of energy folded around her hull.

She was not even frightened. She was numb. She did not know whether Trammerden would keep his promise, or whether she would. How could she remain silent about something like this? And would the Senior Admin kill them all, anyway, just to make sure?

The energy envelope about her ship met and passed through the field barrier that kept the launch bay and deep space discrete, like a bubble passing through a film of soap; her ship touched down on the skids and slid forward. A small crowd of people stood waiting on the platform.

When she saw the people, fear came. She opened her cockpit hatch and removed her helmet and cap. Her braid tumbled down over her shoulder. She undid her braid clip, shook her hair free, and climbed down the handholds in the hull.

Her teammates were arriving behind her. Several skids down, a nickel-seat cruiser's airlock door was opening. Linc and several seniors walked down its ramp as Andrea jumped down from her own little penny-seater.

Trammerden and two security robots approached her. Four other security robots stood by the bay entry — weapons ready. The implications were not lost on Andrea.

Trammerden glanced in Linc's direction; Andrea cast a desperate glance toward her old friend.

Trammerden grasped her arm, roughly, and pressed his lips against her ear. "His life, and everyone else's in this room, depends on your actions, Colleague. Remember your promise."

Andrea stared at him. Then he stood back, as Linc neared.

Linc's face was lined with concern. "What's the emergency, Tram? We weren't quite finished when you called us back. . . ."

"Your protégé turned rogue," Trammerden said bluntly.

Andrea looked at Trammerden. So that was his plan. Arrest her as a rogue and put her in isolation as he had Jason. But he could not keep Linc out of Security for long. Linc would petition the Collegium Council, if he had to. *I have to make him understand something's wrong,* she thought.

Linc gave Andrea a shocked look. The other team's four ships were coasting to a stop behind her; she heard the squeal of their traces on the skids. Linc turned to Andrea.

"Is this true?" he asked. She stared hard at him but kept her face blank of emotion.

"I had my reasons," she said, and then caught Trammerden's warning glare.

"Why?" Linc asked softly, with a puzzled frown, and touched her arm. She glanced at Trammerden again, then lifted a shoulder.

"I changed my mind about being a pilot."

"You what?" Linc grabbed her shoulders and lifted her onto her toes. "Andy, you never turn rogue in the middle of a run! Never. Are you crazy?"

She lowered her gaze and said nothing. Trammerden pulled Linc back. By this time she was surrounded by all her classmates, a couple of professors, staff members, and assorted other personnel. Victoria had just come up behind Linc; she scowled first at Andrea and then at the two men, her broad, dark face deeply lined. Beside her, a still-helmeted Paul was staring at Andrea, wide-eyed, his face a complex mix of emotions.

Andrea turned to the Senior Administrator. "Let's get this over with," she said. "Sir." She put as much contempt as she dared into the honorific. Trammerden gave her a long, considering look. A nasty smile came onto his face.

"Pilot Ito, you did not simply rogue in the middle of a run — you forced your classmates to do likewise. Collegium has no room for people like you." He stepped forward and ripped the chevrons from Andrea's tunic. "You are expelled."

Andrea gave him her coldest stare. Then she

nodded with exaggerated courtesy. "Thank you, Senior Colleague."

Trammerden gave her the hint of a bow; a brief glimmer of rather surprised respect had come into his eyes. Then he waved his security robots forward; they locked titanium claws about her forearms. Linc stepped forward.

"Now wait a minute, Tram. . . ."

Tram spun on him. "Standard procedure, Colleague."

Linc laughed harshly, shook his head. "Uh-uh, Trammerden. You put her under arrest, and I'll have you before the Collegium Council in no time."

Tram raised a single eyebrow. "You do that, Colleague. Your protest has been noted. But I wouldn't make too much noise, if your promotion means anything to you."

He turned his back on Linc. Linc glared at him for a moment, then turned and stalked angrily away. The robots led Andrea out.

Jason watched them bring her in, through the clear field of his cell door. Her oval face was haggard, her lips thin. She stumbled, then tossed her hair out of her face with a glare at the automaton that tugged insistently on her arm.

"Are you all right?" he asked. Her hollow gaze locked with Jason's, over the shoulder of the automaton. She nodded.

"For the moment," she said wearily. Then they led her out of his range of vision, toward the cell next to his.

After the two security robots had left, leaving only the guard robot behind, he pressed his cheek against the door. "Andrea?"

Her voice drifted around the corner, distorted and muted by the energy doors.

"Jason." Her voice quavered. "I got your message. We aborted. Both teams. He's stopped. We stopped him."

Jason sank against the wall. Relief made his knees nearly buckle. He laid his palm against the wall. "Sssrei, we did it. Andrea did it."

"You stopped him," he said aloud. She had gotten his message and believed him.

Sssrei, outside in the corridor, flooded his senses with elation. "And my people . . ."

". . . will have their 'companions,'" Jason returned. It was almost over. Tram was defeated.

"I can't hear you, Jason." There was panic in Andrea's voice.

"I said you stopped him," he repeated more loudly. "The Commonwealth and the Aggregate are alerted now. They'll send help."

There was no reply.

"Andy?"

"Jason . . ." Her voice was choked, as though she were crying. "There won't be any help. He said he'd kill you and Linc if I didn't cooperate. No one knows. No one." Her voice died away.

"What does she mean?" Sssrei transmitted uneasily.

"It's not quite over with, apparently," Jason responded. "We've put an end to his plans but we still have to deal with him. He still has the might of Collegium at his disposal, and he hasn't given up yet."

"What shall we do?"

"I'm thinking," Jason thought in reply. "Tram's going to hear this, but I don't see any other way."

He said aloud, "'Andrea, are you still listening?"

"I'm listening." Her voice was flat.

"Is there anyone out there, anyone in Collegium who would believe us if we told them what was going on?"

"And just how are we going to contact anyone from in here?" she asked. "Charge the door?"

Jason grinned wryly. "I already tried that. It didn't work."

She was silent.

"Can you think of anyone?" he asked.

"No." Her voice was pensive. "I don't know. Maybe Linc, if I could talk to him privately. But there's no way . . ." her voice tapered off.

Andrea lowered her head. Her hair tumbled across her face, screening her suddenly thoughtful expression from the watching cameras.

Several realizations had just struck her, in rapid sequence. Jason had already gotten one message out — he had a telepathic alien friend who could use a computer. According to Victoria, Weasel had flashed to what was happening. And thrideotapes were recording their every word and facial expression in 3-D, for Trammerden's leisurely perusal.

Switch on your scanners, Ito, she thought to herself. Stop being a wipe.

Andrea had remained silent for several seconds. Nothing for it, Jason thought. Trammerden already knows I have a clandestine comm line. I'll have to tell her more and simply avoid specifics.

As he opened his mouth, Andrea said, "I just realized how you got that message out, Jason. You set up a time-delayed message on my terminal that night, didn't you? I thought that was an odd request. I should have flashed then."

Jason was briefly confused, then exultant. He had never asked to use her terminal; he had not even known Tram's scheme then. She was giving him cover.

But his expression did not change. "I wanted a back-up," he said. "In case Tram caught me."

"Guess it was a good thing you did," she said. She paused. "Wish you'd've told me then."

That was from the heart; Jason could hear it in her voice. "I had no proof," he replied. "I didn't figure you'd believe me." I didn't know what he was about to attempt, then. And I didn't know who I could trust.

"Would you have?" he asked.

"No. Probably not." That was also from the heart. Jason leaned his head against the wall with a smile. "It probably sounded pretty outrageous," he said.

"You can believe it." He heard the answering smile in her voice. "So. Yeah, I think someone might believe us, with some persuasion." Jason had the feeling she had someone in particular in mind, but she did not want to say his or her name. "But it's rather a moot question," she added. "We aren't going to be contacting anyone in a hurry."

Jason muttered an absentminded agreement. She had mentioned Linc once already; it had to be him. Jason recreated the lanky commander's image in his mind.

"Think you can find him, Sssrei?"

"I'll find him." The alien's mind-voice was hard. It started away.

"I'm really worried about my colleagues," she said after a pause. "I might have put them in trouble. Especially Paul. He got in on a stipend and can't afford to be expelled. His father would disown him. And Victoria — she's worked so hard. But especially Paul. I feel personally responsible for him."

"I know what you mean," Jason remarked, but he was suddenly confused. Was she telling him to contact her classmates or expressing real regret? "What about your commander friend, Turin? Do you figure he's in any danger?"

"He can take care of himself," she said simply. "Linc's like a cat, he always lands on his feet."

Trammerden had just blackmailed her with the commander's life — Jason knew she was gravely worried about him. So her words were a tracer. She wanted Sssrei to contact Paul.

"Sssrei — wait!"

He sensed the Shenn pause on the periphery of his range. It immediately plucked Paul's and Victoria's images from Jason's mind.

Then its presence was gone. Jason leaned back against the wall and released his breath. "Well," he said, "I guess all we can really do is wait."

"Any chance we'll get word to anyone?"

"Believe it," he said. Confirmation: Sssrei was on its way.

Victoria and her classmates sat in the rec center. The thridy covering the far wall showed an old flatsy movie with the sound turned off. The Hammer had sent them here, after Andrea had been taken away.

Andrea Ito had turned rogue.

Victoria was furious with Andrea, but mostly she was scared. She, too, had aborted the exercise. The Hammer might expel her.

Abruptly she rose to her feet and started pacing. Weasel was eyeing her darkly; he had not spoken since they had received Ito's message, when he had supported its truth and urgency. Everyone else sat with their eyes lowered.

Peace delegates. Impossible.

Well, she could not blame Weasel; it had been her decision.

Victoria paused. Her nagging fear was that Andrea had not been lying to her because she'd twitched, but that she had stripped out completely. There was a chance that Andrea had gone mad.

No. Andrea had not had her wires stripped. She had rogued. She had used their friendship to turn Victoria rogue as well. Trammerden would not have arrested Andrea if she had been right about the foxes being peace delegates.

Victoria grumbled under her breath and resumed her pacing. She should not have heeded Andrea's message. But Weasel had supported Andrea . . . and Victoria had trusted her.

Victoria looked around at her classmates. Only long habit kept her from raging in front of them.

Why did it have to happen to me?

She wanted to smash things — no; she wanted to run hard and fast, as far away from this disaster as she could.

The others were as distressed as she.

"This is a real mess," she said. "But none of you is going to get into trouble, so just stay chill. Andy's going to take the heat, and maybe me. You guys were just following orders." Her glance slid over Weasel; he was still looking at her with an odd expression.

"We're all hurting about Andy," she went on. The words, as she spoke them, cut her like knives. "We've all come through a lot together, and I don't know about the rest of you, but I'm feeling pretty betrayed by what she's done." She hesitated. "People do turn rogue. The thing is, the rest of us have to track together. Right?"

They looked at her.

"Right?" she repeated. They murmured agreement, all but Paul. She glared at him; he said suddenly, "Let's listen to some music."

Ignoring the protests, he jumped up and turned on loud music. Then he pulled Victoria aside and said into her ear, "I don't know what's going on, Vic, but Andy was right. Remember that newsfax I told you about a few weeks ago? About the peace conference on Ceres?"

She gazed at him coolly, without speaking. He released her arm.

"Something strange is going on, carita," he insisted. "I thought nothing about it at the time, but while I was on duty in the newsfax center that day, the printer stopped working after the first few copies were printed out. I called the repair crew, and while they were working on the printer, the Senior Administrator came in and relieved me — almost two hours early. The newsfaxes everyone else read said nothing about the peace conference. Why, Vic? Doesn't that strike you as odd?"

Victoria gave him a look of disgusted incredulity. "You've been watching too many movies, Weasel. Face it. Ito twitched out. She was afraid of getting killed. The Hammer told us it would be especially dangerous. She was afraid, and she twitched." Victoria said it flatly. "That's all there is to it."

"But what about the fax I saw? How do you explain that?"

Victoria shrugged. "I can't explain it. So I suggest we wait until the Hammer gets here and let him explain things. There's got to be a good explanation — and I'm not going to start looking for conspiracies and cover-ups. We have enough trouble without that."

Paul gazed at her for a moment without speaking, then sighed in exasperation, and threw himself down on the cushions. Someone turned down the music.

The others were talking now, Victoria saw. She sat down. Trammerden or one of his mints would show up eventually and tell them what would happen to them.

The person who showed up, though, was Commander Turin. He strode into the room, scanned those present, and spotted Victoria. He motioned to her and took her over to the game tables.

"Colleague Jamison." His dark eyes were probing. "'Tell me what happened out there."

Victoria gazed at him frankly. "Sir, I know who you are, but the Hammer told us we weren't to talk to anyone until he returned."

"Tram was referring to your classmates," he said. "Not to myself."

"I'm not so sure of that, Colleague."

The tall man seemed exasperated; he pursed his lips, studying her.

"Look. You're a friend of Andy's, aren't you?"

"Yes," she said. I was, she thought.

"Then tell me. Has she ever impressed you as a potential rogue?"

Victoria frowned. "It happens. It could happen to anyone. She's always been secretive, Commander. And she's been acting strangely, even before they arrested her boyfriend."

He rubbed at his chin. "Colleague Jamison," he said, "I have been outsystem for the last eight stay-years . . ."

"I'm aware of that."

". . . and I'm speaking from experience when I say that there are times when a commander must choose to disobey a direct order. That's not roguing; it's common sense."

Victoria held his gaze. "Commander, whatever you may think, I'm fully aware of a squad leader's need to make decisions based on information his or her superiors don't have. But this was a programmed exercise, not a real mission. Andrea could only have one reason for aborting the exercise. She twitched."

Weasel had come up to join them. "Andy wouldn't turn rogue. She'd tracked onto something, Vic. I wish you'd listen."

Victoria threw him a warning look. The commander looked at both of them with a thoughtful expression.

"Commander," Victoria said, "I'm sorry. But I have my orders."

Paul stalked over to the thrideo game machines. Turin studied Victoria for another moment, eyebrows elevated. Finally, he nodded.

"Very well. I can respect your position, Colleague. I suppose I'll have to go to the source."

He turned on his heel and left. With a sigh, Victoria collapsed into a cushion. Nothing like facing down a Collegiate commander to make a good day great.

Thomas, across from her, pointed toward the entrance with a nervous laugh. "Look, guys."

She turned. The little alien Andrea had been taking care of was at the duty roster console by the door. It must have entered when the commander left. Thomas walked over to watch it play around with the terminal.

Victoria slumped back into the translucent gel cushions. I think I'll start a fast-food chain, she thought sourly.

"Hey Jamison, come look."

"What?" she asked over her shoulder.

"Come look; it knows how to use a computer."

"Nah. I saw it doing that before," Anya told him. "It's like a monkey. It just writes garbage."

"Some garbage." Thomas's voice sounded strange, but Victoria did not feel like getting up to see.

Rogue-friend, she thought. She stole a glance at Paul. I wonder if roguery is an infectious disease. Everyone seems to be coming down with it. Even good old reliable Weasel is out of control.

"I think it wants you, Paul," Thomas said.

Something in Thomas's voice made Victoria turn. He stood with his hands on his hips, his back to her, blocking her view of the terminal. The alien's tendrils were barely visible above Thomas's right shoulder. Paul had not heard — or had chosen to ignore — Thomas's remark.

Victoria got up and went over. She looked at the screen . . . and her mouth fell open. The alien had purged the screen of its contents and typed in ANDREA'S LIFE IN EXTREME DANGER URGENT SUMMON WEASEL

Victoria turned around. "You might be interested in this, y la Vega."

Paul looked over his shoulder at her. His tone was less than civil. "What do you want?"

Victoria gestured at the screen. "Come see for yourself."

His expression changed when he read the screen. His eyes grew wide; his face went ashen and taut. He eyed the alien, which was still typing, slowly.

"I don't understand," he said finally. Victoria thought that was quite an understatement.

Nöel came up behind Weasel and scanned the screen. She scowled. "This somebody's idea of a joke?" she demanded.

"I stood right here and watched it," Thomas said. Weasel said nothing. The creature's fibers moved about at them all, then returned to point toward the screen.

It typed while they watched. The words were a long time coming.

I HAVE BEEN SENT TO GIVE YOU A MESSAGE. I AM SSSREI, AN INTELLIGENT BEING AND FRIEND OF JASON AND ANDREA.

Everyone gathered around. As it continued to type, their murmurs died away to stunned silence. Finally the creature finished.

Paul turned to Victoria. There was vindication, as well as shock, in his gaze. "Makes sense, carita," he said softly. "Only thing that does."

Victoria motioned Weasel to silence, turned to François and gestured for him to turn up the music.

When she looked around at them all, her expression was grim. "Looks like we need to touch heads," she said.

Something decidedly odd was going on, and Commander David Turin was not going to see Andrea's career ruined without a fight.

He had left the rec center because he could think of no rejoinder to Victoria's position. It was his own. Hard as it was to accept, there could be no good reason for Andrea to abort the exercises. But Trammerden was way out of line, and Linc was not about to let the matter rest.

First he went to Security. As he had expected, Trammerden had put the area under no-access. But there were always alternative courses of action. Linc had a few connections with the Collegium Administration back in Rio de Janeiro.

His own ship, a nickel-seat Suzuki scout, did not have a radio with a long enough range to reach the Collegium Council on Earth. But the school's drone ships had all been equipped with tolyernet transmitters several years before.

Linc activated a school map hologram in the lounge down the hall from Security. The computer scanned onto the location of the drone launch bay. Finally the module he sought appeared. Linc leaned forward to study the projection.

The drone launch bay was on minimal life support; chill drafts coursed through the corridors and floor lights were the only illumination as Linc made his way through the dark halls.

Surprise — the door was locked. Linc's eyes

narrowed. Why should the launch bay be off-limits? What was Trammerden up to?

At that instant the door shimmered open. Linc ducked back into the shadows. A robot whispered past him on a cushion of air. Linc waited for it to pass, then dove for the door, pushing his way through its energy field as it solidified. He crouched inside the bay, skin stinging, and looked around.

Obscured by the dim hulks of the drone ships was a pool of light. Linc heard scraping sounds and a voice. Tram's voice. Phantom-quiet, Linc crept closer.

From behind a bulkhead, he watched for several minutes without understanding. Trammerden was directing a number of automatons which were clustered around a human-sized, cylindrical object. Behind them was the open airlock to a drone ship. Linc could not tell what the cylindrical object was; the lights were behind it and the robots blocked his view.

There was no way he could safely move closer — it looked like it was time to take a calculated risk. Linc moved swiftly across the open space and ducked beneath the drone. Tram hadn't seen him; the other man's attention was focused on a magnetic containment box one of his robots was lowering into the opening. A surgeon robot? This grew more and more interesting.

"Carefully now," Trammerden was murmuring. There was fear in the administrator's voice as he stared at the box. Linc wondered what could make Trammerden so nervous. Now that he was closer, Linc realized what the cylinder was. It was a warhead. And the magnetic containment box — Trammerden was arming an antimatter bomb with enough antihydrogen to wipe out an entire colony.

He must have made a sound. Trammerden spun; their gazes met. Tram had a maser pistol pointed at Linc's head. Molten metal from the belly of the drone spattered only centimeters from his temple. Linc dove, came up running on the far side of the drone. He heard Trammerden shouting — robots blocked the path to the door. He leaped over them — agony seared into him. He was hit. He struck the floor, screaming.

Trammerden was looking down at him.

"Toss him out an airlock," he said to the robots.

Linc was swept up in a tidal wave of white pain as the robots lifted him in their metal arms.

Chapter 17

Jason woke abruptly from a deep sleep. Exhaustion had caught up with him after Sssrei left. He had told Andrea to wake him in about an hour. It did not feel as though he had slept for more than a couple of minutes. He sat up, yawned, and stretched.

Trammerden stood outside the door, watching him. Jason's mouth closed in midyawn. "I wondered when you'd show up," he said.

Tram lifted his eyebrows with a sardonic smile. "I see you've recovered." He came into the cell; the butt of a maser pistol jutted from his holster. "There has been a delay in my plans; I've been rather busy."

"Delay?" Jason swung his legs over the edge of the bed and laughed. "Your arrogance is incredible. Don't you ever learn? We stopped you. The delegates are safely on Ceres. The news media is out in full force. There's not a thing you can do, Tram. You're finished."

Tram smiled indulgently. "A two hundred megaton antimatter bomb dropped on Ceres will have the same effect as the destruction of the convoys. Though with greater loss of life, regrettably. That's not what I came here to talk about, though. I'm more interested in talking about you."

"Are you?"

Trammerden leaned against the wall. "Indeed. You pose a real mystery. My projections and plans included every contingent but your reappearance." He eyed Jason narrowly. "I suspect that you might be useful to me. . . ."

Jason rested his elbows on his knees. "Get to the point, Tram. Your presence is becoming tedious."

The corners of Trammerden's lips turned up while he studied Jason. "I think I'll change my plans regarding you, Jason. I intended to force you to tell me how you got here and how you learned about my plans — and failing that, to kill you. But I think not." Then the chronometer on his wrist hummed. He touched it, read its display, and frowned.

"Impossible. How could they have guessed so soon?" He looked up at Jason, and a speculative, almost suspicious, light grew in his eyes. "I'll wager you had something to do with this."

He waved the automaton over to open the field door for him. Jason rushed to the door as Trammerden hurried into the hall.

"Andrea?"

Andrea's voice came to him. "Jason — are you chill?"

Jason's brow creased. "Kelvin zero. Just a little confused."

"What happened?"

"I'm not sure. He started talking about how I might fit into his plans. I think his wires are totally stripped." Jason hesitated. "Something called him away."

Suddenly, Victoria, Paul, and several other armed cadets burst into the foreroom. The guard robot approached them with its laser arm extended. Paul dodged a burst of crimson brilliance and fired back sound waves with his sonic rifle. The automaton hissed to a halt, belching smoke, and settled to the floor. Victoria, grinning, gave him a slap on the back. Then they looked at Jason and Andrea.

"You two are quite a sight," Weasel said.

Andrea's tone was dry. "How about action first and talk later? I'm getting claustrophobic."

"If you insist." Victoria walked over to the control panel between the two cells. In seconds they were freed.

Jason stepped into the foreroom just in time to see Sssrei roll inside. With a cry of relief, he ran and scooped the little Shenn into his arms. Its filaments touched his face and neck.

"I feared we would be too late."

"Your timing was perfect, friend." Jason glanced back at Andrea, who was conferring with Victoria and Paul. "What's happening?"

"I am uncertain — I cannot read their thoughts and there has been no time for written communication."

Jason walked up to them, Sssrei tucked under his arm. Paul handed him a sonic pistol; Jason nodded thanks.

"No one has seen Commander Turin anywhere," Victoria was telling Andrea. "He may have been locked up with the staff. I'll have someone check."

"Thanks. He'll support us once he knows what's happening, and we're going to need some admin backup before this is all over." Andrea glanced at Jason; there was worry in her eyes.

"What did you guys do that shook Trammerden up so badly?" Jason asked.

Paul smiled, a predator's grin. "We're staging a mutiny." At Jason's amazed stare, he said, "We don't know who Trammerden's accomplices are, so we decided to take over the entire school. We've locked up all the members of the staff and the professors and most of the support personnel. There's been only minimal resistance so far," he told Andrea. "No serious injuries."

Andrea nodded. "Good. What's the status on the Hammer?"

Victoria shook her head, grimly. "Haven't been able to locate him. And there are a couple of other problems — all elevator systems are shut down, so we can't get to the comm center. And the launch bay and dry docks are all sealed."

Andrea was concerned. "That is a problem; we need the comm center, or else we're cut off. The Hammer may have us beat if we can't get word out before he makes a move against us."

"We have a bigger problem than that," Jason said. The others looked at him. "I think Trammerden has launched a drone convoy to bomb Ceres."

Andrea's eyes widened. "Come on," she said.

"Victoria, you organize a search for Trammerden. Thomas, get to work on breaking into the launch bay. Paul, raise a cadre of twenty and meet Jason and me in the senior lounge."

They left security at a dead run.

Andrea, Paul, Thomas, Simon, and several others gathered around a hologram of the comm module, pointing and arguing. Jason was perched on a table to one side with Sssrei in his lap, giving the discussion only half of his attention.

Tram was not going to be that easy to find. He was dead certain of it. The man was hiding somewhere; he would have prepared for this contingency. Trammerden was always prepared.

"Why not climb one of the elevator shafts?" Paul suggested.

"Why not climb *all* of them?" Thomas pointed out. "That way, even if they're armed, we can take them without too many casualties."

"I don't want any casualties," Andrea said. "We're not fighting a war here. We're probably dealing with a group of frightened people who have heard that the students are running amok and they don't know what to do about it."

"Unless they're Trammerden's people," Simon said.

"No." The others turned at the flat certainty in Jason's voice. He shook his head. "No. They're not. It's not Trammerden's style."

"Who made you the expert on Jon Trammerden?" Simon asked Jason. Something in Jason's gaze, though, brought a flicker of discomfort to Simon's eyes, and he looked away.

Andrea was squinting at the projection of the comm center, tracing the entry locations, which were displayed in bright red. "No good, no good. The comm personnel may not be trained, but all they have to do is stand at the elevator terminals with heavy objects and club our people as they climb out."

Then, as she stared, a slow gleam came into her eyes. She touched Paul's arm and said, "Weasel. Simon. What's the big problem with hitting the comm center right now? Tactically."

Simon and Paul glanced at each other, eyeing the projection.

"We can't get in quickly enough to overwhelm them," Simon said.

"Yes? And?"

Paul was looking at Andrea now, his dark eyes mere slits. "It's uphill for us, through a narrow passage," he said. A smile came onto Andrea's face.

"Exactly. So all we have to do is make it not uphill."

Jason, off to one side, was the first to flash to what she was saying. He nodded and shared amusement with Sssrei, who was also listening to the exchange.

Paul's eyes widened. "Shut down the grav-field generator?"

She nodded and pointed. "The power source for the generator is in module 4 — there's easy access to it."

"Clever," Simon said. He was nodding thoughtfully. "But they'll still be able to fight us in null grav. It might be a better idea to overload the generator and create an artificial gee-hole; we can take advantage of their disorientation."

Jason had studied the concept in Field Theory. Artificial gravity generators were strange and sensitive beasts: give them too much power, and they went wild, radiating spasms of shifting gravity that wrought havoc.

"Uh-uh." Andrea shook her head. "Too violent. It'd destroy machinery and cause injuries all over the school. Besides, those people aren't trained in null-grav fighting. Shut off the generator, and they'll be helpless. We'll have them."

After a pause, Simon nodded. "Yeah. It just might work."

Paul let out a whoop and slapped his thigh. "*Might* work? It's brilliant! Compadres, we have ourselves a plan!"

Andrea's chronometer buzzed. It was Victoria.

"Andy, I think. . . ." There was a pause. "We need you down here."

Jason's heartrate leapt; he straightened. Had they found Tram already?

Andrea frowned. "Where are you? What's going on?"

"Module 61, airlock antechamber. We found Commander Turin."

"Terrific! Put him on."

The silence lengthened. Jason watched an

impassive mask slide down over Andrea's face. Her tone was flat. "He's been injured, hasn't he?" she asked.

"Umm," Victoria's voice wavered and rose slightly in pitch. "I don't want you to be alarmed. . . ."

"I'm on my way."

Andrea threw a look back at Jason. Her eyes were the only thing alive on her face, and they were screaming. He was on his feet instantly.

"Paul, you're in charge till I get back," she said. Her voice was almost normal. "Get the comm center for me, Weasel. We're running out of time."

"You got it, carita."

She was out the door before Paul finished speaking, with Jason and Sssrei behind her.

Jason had a hard time keeping up with Andrea, who wove through the corridors at a run, barely avoiding collisions with the students roaming the halls. Jason dodged around them, shielding Sssrei with an arm. He caught up with Andrea at the entrance to a room and looked over her shoulder.

The commander lay prone on the floor in the antechamber to a module airlock. A deep, blackened gouge was sliced deep into his back. Victoria and François stood by the body. When Andrea entered the room, Victoria gave François a nod; he took his search team and left.

Andrea walked forward slowly, hands clenched. She stopped, knelt beside Turin, and pressed her fingers against his neck. Jason squatted next to her. She looked at him.

"No pulse," she said calmly. "He's dead." Her face was totally expressionless. Jason repressed a shudder.

He sensed Sssrei's curiosity and sorrow, as it regarded Turin's body. "This is a dead human? We are too alike in death, our peoples."

"They saved me, and I was as dead as he is." Jason stood. "We need a physician."

Victoria nodded. "Talies is on her way."

Moments later Dr. Talies entered with two med techs and a life-saving unit. Turin's body was gently lifted and lowered into the cylindrical coffin. Talies leaned in to insert needles and attach electrodes. Then she had the med techs close the lid and checked the readings.

Jason put an arm around Andrea's shoulder. She did not respond to his touch. "Well?" she asked.

Dr. Talies straightened, met Andrea's gaze, and spread her hands.

"I can't say till I get him back to the med center and examine him. "We can revive him, keep him alive, and get him to a hospital back on Earth. But if he was dead too long, the brain cells — "

"I know that." Andrea was impatient. "Go. Get to work on him. Don't waste time."

She spun to Victoria. "Keep searching. Find Trammerden."

Jason preceded her out the door. She stood in the middle of the corridor, staring after the techs who took Turin away, until Jason took her arm and turned her to face him. She wrenched herself free; her eyes blazed at him, furnace hot, for an instant. Then the mask snapped back into place.

"Let's get back to Weasel," she said. They started working their way back.

They lost gravity as they neared the communication module. Startled, Jason lost his grip on Sssrei. The little alien floated out of his arms. He grabbed Sssrei and tucked it under his arm.

Gravity was restored only moments later; from the voices on Andrea's chronometer, Jason gathered that the battle for control of the comm center had been successful. The comm personnel were unarmed, untrained, and could not begin to compete with the students in null-grav fighting. They received word that the lifts were working again. They entered an elevator and headed up.

When the elevator reached its destination, Jason stepped out behind Andrea. The increased gee-force tugged at his limbs and pulled at the muscles of his face and chest.

"You're putting on weight, Sssrei," he thought, shifting to get a better hold on it. Sssrei's fibers were extended to their full length; he sensed its presence in his mind. It was looking upward, awed. Jason looked around, and his mouth fell open.

Collegium's control center was the largest single chamber in the school. It took up an entire module. Spherical, it was about half a kilometer in diameter. Scattered clusters of command centers spread out around Jason, but most were deserted. As his gaze followed the curve of the module, he saw armed students walking up and down the walls, like flies, and hanging upside down from the distant ceiling. Jason looked down at his feet, queasy.

Weasel and Simon had joined them; Simon came up to Jason while Weasel spoke with Andrea. "It affected me the same way, the first time," Simon said, grinning. "Come on."

Jason trailed him and the others through the banks of machinery. He was chill as long as he did not look up too high.

They approached one of the command centers, where a knot of students stood. Jason looked back the way they had come. The elevator terminal was a quarter of the way up the curved wall. Jason tried not to think about it.

Several physics seniors with sonic weapons guarded the comm personnel, who lay face down on the floor in front of the semi-circle of comm equipment. The head engineer, a sixty-year-old man, was bound to his chair with energy snakes. He looked extremely angry.

"Will someone tell me what's going on?" he demanded of them. Andrea bent over him to examine the comm screens.

"Everything's shut down," Weasel said. "No telemetry at all."

"I could have told you that," the head comm engineer snapped. "Orders of the Senior Administrator."

Andrea grabbed his arms. Her expression made him pale. "You have to turn it back on. It's urgent."

"They're installing a new set of commware;

the old system has been almost totally disassembled." He added, belligerent, "That's what I was told. Honestly, Colleague, I simply do my job. It's been out for hours."

"Where are the installation personnel, then? Where's the new equipment?"

The older man returned her stare. Simon, beside Jason, murmured in tones of purest disgust, "Drone."

"Nöel is good with computers," Weasel said. Andrea nodded.

"Call her. And tell her to hurry."

She arrived within moments of their summons. Jason had never seen her before. She was a young girl with stringy, pale blond hair down to her shoulders, all bones and angles, and looked more like an orphan than an engineering senior. She approached them, with her feral, violet eyes darting, and went to Andrea and Weasel.

Weasel explained what they needed. She nodded sharply and sat down at the console next to the head comm engineer. Her hands flitted over the controls. After a few moments of tense silence, she turned to Andrea, looking exasperated.

"Can't do it quickly. Software's too tight. Take days."

Andrea nodded toward the console. "Keep trying."

It became obvious that the outgoing comm lines would not be up soon. Jason settled into a chair and watched as Andrea began to pace, knotted with suppressed energy.

Dr. Talies contacted them. "Colleague Ito?"

Andrea dove for the console. "Here."

"We've finished our scan. I think we got to him in time, Colleague. He's still in danger — but he's alive. I wanted to let you know. I'm going to begin prepping him for the trip to Earth."

"He won't be going anywhere if we don't get through to Ceres," Andrea said. Then she shook her head. "Thank you, doctor." She glanced at Jason; life had come back into her face. A brief smile passed between them.

Weasel relayed a status report from Victoria. "No sign of Trammerden, and they've pretty much covered the entire school."

"There are a lot more people looking for him than there are places to hide," she said. "Where could he be?"

Weasel shrugged eloquently.

Andrea turned to Jason. She had a pensive look on her face. "Weasel," she said over her shoulder, "Keep things under control here. Jason and I are going to help Victoria's search."

Jason followed Andrea back to the elevator, mystified. It was clear from her expression that she had had a thought. But she shook her head at Jason's questioning look. They descended in silence.

The elevator door slid open. They exited and passed several roving bands of cadets, who waved at them and called greetings. They sure are enjoying this, Jason thought. Broken hulks of maintenance and housekeeping robots littered the corridors and passages; some excesses were taking place.

Andrea led him to the gauntlet gym's control room. She bent over the console.

Jason raised his eyebrows; she was depressurizing the gym. Then he understood. He went down to the first level, set Sssrei down, and pulled a couple of pressure suits out of the locker, checking them quickly.

Andrea joined him. They suited up outside the room and wrapped energy envelopes about themselves with the suits' controls. Then they passed through the door into the airless room. Jason adjusted his temp controls.

"Shut off your radio," Andrea's voice said in his ear. He did so; she took him by the arms and pressed her face plate against his.

"This may be paranoid," she said. Jason grinned at her. He could see her dark eyes and answering smile through the layers of plasteen that separated them.

"It's hard to be too paranoid with Tram," he replied. "What are you thinking?"

"I'm thinking," she said, "that he couldn't have pulled all this off without everyone knowing unless he had someplace, some control center of his own no one knew about." She paused, chewing her lip. "Is it possible there's a module around that we don't know about? One that used to be in use but was shut down?"

"Yeah, it's possible. The only way we could find it would be to search Collegium on the outside and see if all the modules match the maps."

"Then let's do it," Andrea said. "He may see

us coming, but maybe he won't realize what we're doing."

They reactivated their envelopes and exited the gym, not bothering to unsuit.

Jason picked up Sssrei, then caught up with Andrea out in the hall. Eventually they reached the tunnel. It stretched before them, and then curved up.

They passed beneath the lounge module and reached the bottom of the tunnel that climbed up along its side. Jason looked around for cam-I's; there were none in the lounge. Best they hurry, anyhow. Andrea turned on the electromagnets on her palms and feet, and started up. Jason gave her a couple seconds, then started up after her.

A shadow crossed Jason's face. He looked upward, through the lounge. Beyond the clear dome of the lounge, the cannibalized wheel of the old school partly obscured the distant sun.

His heartrate sped up. Can't tell Andrea till we're outside, he thought. But he knew.

Sssrei's filaments followed his gaze. "Take me with you," it said. Jason was surprised.

"Why?"

"Because if all else fails, I can destroy his mind."

"Your restraints. . . ."

"I'll overcome them, somehow." But the alien's thoughts leaked doubt. "I might be of some use," it insisted.

Jason shook his head. "Sssrei, I've already put you in too much danger. You are your people's only representative. I'm going to leave you with Andrea. You're too valuable to lose."

"The choice is mine." Sssrei's tone was final. "Respect our friendship enough to allow me that choice."

Andrea had climbed out into the observatory, a mini-globe that nestled against the side of the lounge module like a wart. Unlike the other modules, its skin was a shimmering, matter-repulsive field. The only way through it was by means of an energy envelope.

The gravity here was low. Jason tied himself to one of the power hooks as Andrea was doing. A row of scooters was parked near the edge of the module. The shadow of the old school created sharp lines across the deck.

Jason lowered his face plate. As soon as Andrea followed suit, he pressed his face plate against hers.

"Look toward the sun," he said. Puzzled, she did so. When her gaze returned to Jason's, her eyes were wide.

"I'll be slagged," she said softly.

"I'm going after him."

"*We're* going after him."

Jason shook his head. "The smaller the mass, the better. He's a lot more likely to scan two scooters heading for him than one. You're needed here."

"No way." Her jaw had set.

"Andy, don't get stubborn."

"I'm not the one being stubborn, MacLeod. I'm not going to let you go off on a suicide run."

"It's not a suicide run." Jason released her arms, but kept contact with her face plate.

"Tram wants me alive. If you go, he'll have someone to threaten me with, and I wouldn't be able to stand up against that. You matter to me." It took some doing to get the words out. There was no answering light in her eyes; she gazed at him without expression. "Our only other choice is a frontal assault, and a lot of cadets are going to die that way.

"Give me an hour, Andrea," he said. "Please."

Anger flared in her eyes. "This isn't a game, Jason, and it's not some fantasy duel. That man is dangerous. Look what he did to Linc." Her voice broke. "Jason, he'll kill you, or torture you, or — I don't know what. I'm not going to stay back here wondering whether you're still alive. If you go alone, you're a wolfman. You're rogue. That's all there is to it."

Jason was suddenly angry. "I'm going," he said. "Alone."

She stood back from him and flipped her radio on. Her voice was cold. "Well, happy trails, Wolfman."

She started to leave.

"Andrea," he said. She paused and looked back at him. "Tell them about Sssrei's people and the convolver," he said. Then she was gone.

Sssrei was eyeing him; he sensed its regard.

"She had no right to tell me what to do."

"You allowed me to make my own choice, Jason-human," it said. "Where is the difference?"

Jason glared at Sssrei, then untied himself and started toward the scooters. without bothering to reply.

Chapter 18

The scooters were used for satellite and bulk-head repairs. Jason touched the ignition and the machine came to life.

Sssrei rolled up to join him. He put the alien between his feet under the dash, switched on his suit's field, and altered the setting so that the entire scooter was enveloped. Sssrei's filaments came up over the dash. Their glow created spots of orange light on the tinted screen.

Jason straddled the scooter, gripped the steering bar, pressed the accelerator, and shoved. The scooter skidded off the edge of the module and slid through the energy wall. He scrambled aboard as emptiness fell away beneath him. The rock mazes near Collegium, spirals and clusters of coarse-hewn moons, drifted across the sprinkling of asteroids. Beyond them a trillion stars blazed icy white. The only sound was his breathing.

He looked sunward and steered toward the old Collegium wheel. Earth and Mars, bluish white and rusty, bracketed the sun. Jason had never been that far insystem. He suddenly regretted that fact.

The old Collegium neared quickly. He entered its shadow and headed toward a spot where the antiquated wheel had been stripped of its hull. He had forgotten how big it was.

It was still rotating slowly. There would be some gravity inside then. Seeing it torn apart, huge strips of its dull silver skin peeled back like the rind of some half-eaten fruit, pained Jason. He guided the scooter among the naked girders.

Jason released his breath. He had not known he was holding it. When he saw an intact hallway in front of him, he steered toward it and landed his scooter on its edge. The vehicle skittered along the floor for a meter or so before it stopped. Jason climbed out, moving slowly in the almost negligible gravity, and picked up Sssrei. It was excited and a little awed.

Some distance down the curved corridor, Jason saw faint light and shadow. His heart leapt. Parts of the station were still powered. He propelled himself toward the light along the floor and ceiling of the corridor. Around a sharp curve he passed through an energy wall; sudden gravity slammed him against the floor. He landed in a squat, barely retaining his grip on Sssrei.

An artificial gravity generator. They were nearing Tram's control center.

He was in the old dorm section. The metal walls were covered with ice-coated graffiti — the cadets' departure celebrations must have been wild. Enormous icicles hung from the open doorways and steel rafters, bleeding slow drops of water; fog blanketed the floor. There was obviously some kind of atmosphere.

Jason turned off his field and opened his face plate. There was a faint hiss and his ears crackled from the drop in pressure, but the air was breathable. He pulled off his helmet. The stinging cold on his cheeks and neck made him shiver.

He set Sssrei down. "Be careful," he warned it. "Stay behind me. And at the first sign of trouble make like a weed and roll like crazy. Got it?"

"Of course." Sssrei's reply was distracted. It was looking around. "My people would be amazed," it exclaimed. "What a glorious synthesis of skill and mind our two races would form!"

"This is no time for philosophy." Jason started down the corridor. Sssrei caught up and rolled along at his heels.

"Jason, I've been reflecting."

"No kidding." Jason pulled off his gloves and tucked them into his belt, before checking his maser pistol. Eighty-two percent charged. He velled the gun back onto his belt.

"I am quite serious. I think," it continued as it rolled, "our two peoples are much more similar than I had originally thought."

Jason glanced down at Sssrei. "Don't consider me a representative sample of the human race, friend."

"This is important, Jason. Please be quiet and listen."

Jason was surprised enough at the sharpness in Sssrei's tone to close his mouth on what he had been about to say.

Sssrei pointed its optic fibers at him and went on, "You need to understand more about enemy-bonding. I originally thought of your connection with Trammerden as only loosely like an enemy-bond, but I have begun to think that the similarities are much greater than I had realized. The bond gives Trammerden knowledge of and power over you — "

"I don't want to hear any more of this," Jason interrupted. Sssrei thought-spoke over him, "and it also gives you knowledge of and power over him."

"Shut up!" Jason was starting to get really annoyed. Sssrei was paying no attention, but was going on, "Killing you will be like killing himself, and because of this he will be reluct — "

Two creatures were waiting around the next curve. Jason froze. He had heard a little bit about them. They were straight out of the early days of genetic engineering: a male and a female. Their faces and bodies were humanoid, beautifully proportioned and muscled. They had luxuriant white hair that tumbled down their backs.

Any resemblance to humans ended there. Their skin was a glossy gold. They would have been eight feet tall if they had stood upright; they were both extremely long in the torso and had a pair of apelike arm-legs beneath their normal arms, and short, powerful hind legs.

Homo ingenium — engineered humans. Everyone called them trugs. They had been engineered to work in the asteroids, a failed effort that was outlawed while Jason was attending Collegium. Trugs were bred, according to reports, for long life, docility, strength, and minimal intelligence. Most of them had been shipped back to Earth during the mid-eighties.

They seemed more curious about him than anything else. They sniffed his face and hair, his armpits. Then the male slapped at his own ears and cocked his head. As he looked at Jason the expression on his face changed from simple curiosity to . . . something else.

The male grabbed him with both sets of arms, upended him, and tucked him under his upper right arm. Jason did not even have time to react. Sssrei shouted a useless warning into his mind. Spurred by a surge of adrenaline, Jason struggled, but the arms imprisoning him were as strong as bands of titanium. The male loped down the corridor on three limbs at an alarming rate; Jason, upside down, watched the female lope along behind.

Sssrei was calling out to him. He could not make sense of its thoughts. Guess Tram's discovered me, he thought, and suppressed hysterical laughter.

Don't twitch out, MacLeod. He gave up struggling and concentrated on regaining his calm. He began to recite to himself the stars in Cassiopeia, in order of magnitude.

Eventually the male paused outside an open

doorway. The graffiti by Jason's face read, "ECOSYS ENGINEERS — CLASS OF '99!!" and "Plug into the jjAggWAvE" and, in neat writing, sideways, "People who write on walls are the lowest form of primordial SLIME." The male set him down inside the door. Jason stood.

The room wandered away from him, a labyrinth of crystal, alloy, and light. Prisms and razor-sharp sheets of glass and metal knives sketched mirrored, rainbow designs in the air. It was a puzzle, a fantasy. A deadly one.

Jason blinked, rubbing his eyes. Just looking into the maze made him dizzy. He squinted into the confusion. Trammerden was somewhere in there.

He lifted a foot and the world turned on end. He was suddenly plummeting toward the gleaming edge of a sheet of glass. It would slice him in two. Jason tucked himself into a ball and struck the flat of a metal jag with his outstretched hand as he fell. It deflected him — he shot past the sheet's edge and skidded down the glass surface. The gravity shifted again; Jason sat upright on the transparent surface.

He quickly scanned his surroundings. Glass edges and knives glimmered all about him. The door was tilted sideways now, a dark rectangle about two meters to his left.

Trammerden had set up a second grav generator, contained its field within this room, and powered it to the brink of overload. It teetered on the edge of a gee-hole. The grav orientation had changed twice in an instant. The fluctuations would be truly random; there would be no pattern he could discern and outwit. This was going to be harder than he had thought.

The orientation was wavering enough to make him dizzy, but not enough to pull him from the surface of the glass plane. He sat for several moments, tense, expecting a shift any second. When none came, Jason stood cautiously and took a few wobbling, tentative steps. He was bathed in sweat, his hands were shaking.

Gravity shifted sharply, turning the plane of the glass into a steep incline. Jason struck the surface and slid downward on his belly, clawing for a hold.

An intersecting plane of glass sliced upward along his shin, tearing his pressure suit; Jason grasped its edge with his fingernails and scrambled onto it. He jumped upward and grabbed a horizontal metal beam, swung over it as gravity shifted again, and slid down the now slanting beam. Dropping to another plane of glass, he ran. He was getting the hang of this maze — kept moving, using the grav shifts to his advantage. He would reach the center of this maze eventually — if he could keep himself alive.

He neared and receded from the center three times. There were several close calls, but each time he approached the center the exit was closer. Trammerden was watching — Jason caught glimpses of him between leaps. But the shifting gravity always carried Jason away.

Finally, a break — Jason did a roll, a dash, and struck his shoulder on a floor that had become a wall. He sprang to his feet. He had made it out of the maze. Trammerden stood, arms folded, studying him. The older man was dressed in a simple black flight suit. His expression was indecipherable.

They were in a robotic command center. Banks of lighted machinery murmured and hummed around them; hologram displays and four dimensional maps flickered ghostlike above projection consoles. Jason, reluctantly, was impressed.

"Quite a setup you've got here," Jason said. Trammerden nodded. There was a wry smile on his face.

"Indeed." He gestured toward the banks of machinery. "You'll find equipment here that is used virtually nowhere else in the system."

"I know; I got a look at your purchasing records." Jason pulled his maser free of its velcro holster. Trammerden shook his head.

"That's useless here. Check the charge."

Jason glanced at the gun's LCD; it registered zero. With a shrug he stuck the weapon back onto his belt. He sensed Sssrei, faintly, calling him.

"Here, Sssrei," he thought. "Hurry."

Trammerden had settled into a chair at one of the consoles and regarded Jason. He was talking. ". . . troublesome when we were seniors, Jason, and you're an irritant now. I'm not even certain why I have this impulse not to kill you outright."

Jason shrugged. "Perhaps some vestige of humanity."

Tram's eyes glittered. "Don't test my

patience. You'll find it's not infinite." Then his expression grew thoughtful again. "No, I think it's because I sense a like soul in you. Undeveloped, shackled by inexperience and moral cowardice, perhaps, but I think we're more alike than I would ever have suspected."

The words sank into Jason like teeth. *Enemy-bond.* He gave Trammerden a look of pure hatred. Sssrei's voice whispered into his mind. "I'm outside the door, Jason. Shall I enter?"

"Too dangerous." Jason looked away from Tram to hide the growing gleam in his eyes. "Think I've got an idea, Sssrei. Find a computer terminal."

Tram studied him. "I've studied your profiles, both past and present. You have a striking ability to adapt yourself to changing circumstances. In the interval between 2087 and now you seem to have developed highly specialized abilities. There are even indications that you've developed some form of limited psychic ability.

"Unfortunately your candidate test was not designed to analyze in depth the things I would like to know about you. But we can remedy that in the future."

Jason's chest constricted. Being a guinea pig was more terrifying than dying. "I won't be your laboratory animal. I'm here to finish you, Trammerden. Or die trying."

Trammerden seemed amused. "Of course, that fits with your profile. I can force you, naturally." He touched the arm of his chair and several miniature scenes from the new Collegium appeared before them.

Thomas and a group of engineering seniors were attempting to get through the energy shielding that sealed off the launch bay. In the comm center, Nöel was working at a console. Strands of crimson numbers poured across her screen. At her elbow the holo-table flickered with spectral static.

Jason did not see Andrea in any of the images.

"I could destroy them all at once," Trammerden said, "or in small groups, until you submit. I can shut off their life support, or program the remaining robots to kill them. I'd prefer not to; they will be an invaluable resource in the war.

"But you are more valuable to me. You have an ability I need. So if you force me to, by refusing to cooperate, I will kill every last one of them."

Jason returned his look. "You would, too."

Tram smiled at him. "You begin to understand me."

"Sssrei?"

"I've found a terminal, Jason. What do you want me to do?"

Jason paused. "Sssrei, I want to switch awareness with you. I want you to keep Tram talking while I do a little programming."

Sssrei slid into his body, and he found himself in the Shenn's, outside in the corridor, next to a terminal. In the back of his mind he heard Sssrei prompting Trammerden with questions.

Jason logged into the computer. This computer was linked with the new Collegium banks; his password and user number worked. Good.

Savage delight coursed through him. Trammerden was in for a real surprise.

He wanted to kill Trammerden. It was easier to admit than he would have expected. Sssrei was right — they were bound. To be free of Tram, Jason had to kill him.

It took a while to do what he wanted. When he had finished programming, Jason slipped back into his own body. Trammerden was in midsentence.

". . . mostly scanners. I've put this together with virtually no assistance. Of course, the original construction had to be performed by contractors, but I arranged an accident for them. So no one knows. Except my two bodyguards, whom you've met."

Jason clasped his hands behind his back. Ninety seconds, more or less. One-chimpanzee, two-chimpanzee . . . a red light flickered on Trammerden's panel. Fear walked up Jason's spine. Keep him talking, he thought. "The trugs," he said. "I thought they were all returned to a reservation on Earth."

Trammerden lifted his eyebrows. "I purchased them," he said. "They've turned out to be quite useful."

"It fits." Jason put sarcasm in his tone.

"They're quite intelligent, actually," Trammerden said. "It's their conditioning, and certain drugs, that make these two so cooperative. Modified humans are not drones — the anti-gene engineering fever of the fifties and sixties generated an awful lot of lies and misleading information. The relatives of my two trugs are actually quite articulate and consequently rather difficult to deal with. But I've used various techniques to transform these two into a more useful passivity."

Jason stared at him in horrified disgust. He was not simply amoral; he was a monster. "Nothing is beyond you, is it?"

Trammerden leaned against the panel. "You can't appreciate the necessity, yet. You will eventually, though. I believe you have the capacity to understand and even aid in my plans." His eyes glazed. "When I sabotaged your ship I didn't realize how important a step I had taken. With that one act I cast aside all the rules I was taught in my youth. I realized that I had the ability to reshape destiny."

"I was impressed with your alibi," Jason said. "How did you alter the computer records? I *saw* you enter the launch bay as I was leaving. I knew you slagged some of my navigation microcircuitry; I'd just checked it thoroughly. But the library computer log showed you never left your carrel, and several students swore you were there the whole time."

Tram smiled thinly. "It was quite simple, actually. I wrote a program which continued to input data to the console, so the library log showed I never left the carrel. As for the other students . . ." he shrugged. "They were concentrating on their own studies. And the records showed I couldn't have left. Therefore, I didn't leave. Q.E.D."

"Well planned." Jason was impressed despite

himself. Fifty-two chimpanzee. Fifty-three chimpanzee.

Tram nodded acknowledgement. "I never allow circumstances to rule me. I alter reality to suit my needs." His eyes probed into Jason. "You have that ability as well. I should have realized it years ago, when you did not die. And now, impossibly, you are back. Eventually you will tell me how you did it.

"We are a different kind of human, Jason. Better. More powerful. We can control the future of the human race by the force of our wills. With the proper conditioning, you will make an excellent lieutenant. You will enact my programs, help me remake the future."

"So." Jason's mouth had a vile taste in it. Seventy-chimpanzee . . . seventy-one. He swallowed. "You plan to mold the human race. Like you have your trugs."

"Precisely." Trammerden's eyes narrowed. "Don't look so appalled. Most people are no different from my two friends, anyway. They live out their lives as drones and automatons. They have no control over their fates even now." He grasped Jason's shoulder; Jason turned so that Trammerden could not see the blinking warning light.

"It's a simple matter of evolution, Jason. We're a higher order of human. Most of the race is barely even sentient. Under my rule they will be happy, unified as humankind has never been."

"That says more about you than about the

rest of humanity," Jason said. Eighty-two chimpanzee. He warned Sssrei, pulled loose from Tram's grasp, and wedged himself between two machines.

Then an alarm sounded, a swelling hum. Jason's heartbeat leapt in fear. Trammerden turned his head, surprised; he strode over to the panel.

A hologram glimmered into existence. Andrea had followed him! She had landed where he had and was climbing off her scooter. Then she straightened and checked her weapon. She frowned, velled it to her belt, and looked around. Finally, she pried a long metal rod loose, and began walking.

"Interesting," Trammerden said to himself. "She shows remarkable ingenuity and courage — she might prove useful, as well."

Jason quelled a surge of panic. Hold on, Andrea. Ninety-four-chimpanzee. What was taking so long?

Trammerden turned toward Jason and opened his mouth. Then reality went insane.

Jason clung to the console for his life. Gee-hole. Jason had overloaded Trammerden's state-of-the-art gravity generator. Trammerden was hurled through the air into the maze.

Debris shot about the command center, slamming into the walls, shattering glass in the maze, pulverizing delicate machinery. The power surge would not last long; he had to be prepared.

As quickly as it had begun, it was over. Jason

pried himself free and dashed into the maze after Trammerden.

Tram was crouched nearby, shaking his head. Except for a bleeding cut on his forehead, he was unharmed. He looked up at Jason with glittering eyes. "I'd like to know how you did that," Trammerden grunted. Gravity wobbled about them; they both staggered.

"You're lucky, Tram. That would have killed most people."

Then, as gravity shifted, Jason launched himself. Leopard-swift, Trammerden leapt away and pulled his weapon. Battle was engaged.

Trammerden had a maser, but Jason had logged a lot of sparring hours in the grav gym. He pursued Trammerden through shifting planes of gravity and reflective surfaces, among lethal steel blades and shards of glass; invisible microwave light sizzled around him and ricocheted through the maze. Tram was a fool, using a beam weapon in a mirror maze. He was as likely to hit himself as he was Jason.

Their fight was swift and violent. Jason shot toward Trammerden, struck out with a foot, missed. Gravity reversed its direction while they were both in midair. Jason shoved against a metal edge, slicing his hands open. He jackknifed, and struck Tram's head with both feet.

Luck was in Jason's favor. At that instant a grav shift hurled them both toward the door. Jason smashed his shoulder on the doorjamb and tumbled out into the hall. As he fell sidelong out the door, Jason caught a quick impression of Tram flailing as he smashed into a jagged row of metal teeth on the wall.

Time danced away from Jason. He sat up suddenly — he was still in the hall. Sssrei was at the door to the maze, peering in.

Jason shook his head. The floor was streaked with smears of his blood. He felt faint and sick but was not in pain. Sssrei had dampened his pain centers, he realized.

"How much time?"

"Only seconds. The Trammerden is injured but not mortally. He regains consciousness even now."

Jason forced himself to his feet. The world spun. He staggered to the door. Trammerden was slumped against the wall beside the door, moaning, still gripping his maser.

Gravity shifted — Jason grasped the doorjamb and snatched at Tram's collar as the man rolled sideways above the door. He dragged Tram into the hall and dropped him on the floor. Then Jason pried his fingers loose from the maser pistol.

Jason checked the weapon. Almost fully charged. Trammerden was a bloody mess. His flight suit was shredded; his chest and face were raw; blood dripped from a deep gouge in his throat.

Jason grabbed Trammerden's shirt, lifted him up, and shoved the gun into his ear. Jason's breath was ragged; his pulse pounded in his temples.

"I'm going to kill you, Trammerden," he said.

"You hear me? I'm going to cook your brains."

Trammerden struggled weakly, groaning. For a long moment, with shaking hands, Jason held the gun against the man's ear. Then, with disgust, he clouted Trammerden on the temple with the butt of the gun. Trammerden slumped.

Jason let Trammerden slide to the floor and sat down next to him, drenched in cold sweat. He began to shudder uncontrollably. His throat had closed. He pressed a fist against his temple.

A painful, wrenching sob tore free of his chest, then another, and another. He huddled against his knees and let free a torrent of grief.

Chapter 19

Andrea wandered through the halls, flattening herself against the walls to peer into dark rooms. The place was dead. She had the feeling she was in a ghost station, straight out of an old horror thrideo.

The two modified people she had encountered earlier trailed along behind her. They gave her the creeps; they had not replied to her greeting, but had merely tried to sniff her. After a few tries she had given up trying to communicate with them and had moved on.

Suddenly, the ground was yanked from beneath her feet. Instinctively, she rolled into a ball. Gee forces battered her about the corridor, then, just as abruptly, she was deposited on the floor.

Andrea lay supine, battling nausea and staring blankly at the ceiling. She sat up, shaken but unhurt. At last, she stood and picked up her metal rod. Someone was wreaking havoc with Trammerden's grav generator, and Andrea knew who. She started to run.

Then she heard something. She slowed. The sound came from around the corner. Andrea approached the intersection cautiously, her hands on the metal pipe she carried. She pressed her back against the wall, raised the rod over her head, and peered carefully around the corner. Two pairs of legs were sticking out into the hall. Andrea craned her neck to see more.

Jason looked up at her. His face was blotchy and his eyes swollen. His pressure suit had been badly shredded. He had deep cuts on his face. Andrea saw that the palms of his hands had been sliced to the tendons. Trammerden lay prone beside him.

Andrea gasped. "Is he — ?"

Jason glanced at Tram. His voice was toneless. "No. Only unconscious."

Andrea set her rod down and came around the corner. The Shenn was in the shadows; its filaments and spikes were furled. Andrea knelt beside Jason. He looked at her.

"I couldn't," he said, lowering his head. "I wanted to kill him but I couldn't."

He started to sob. The sobs were dry and weak; no tears came. Andrea took him into her arms. He clung to her. Then he pushed her away. His eyes were haunted.

"He said I was like him. It would have been so easy to kill him." He glanced at Trammerden, and his voice broke. "I wanted to kill him. All this time . . . I kept twitching out to stop myself. I lied to myself. I kept telling myself it was only justice I wanted." Then he fell silent.

Andrea rocked back on her heels and laughed. He looked at her, surprised. "After what he did to you, you're upset for wanting him dead? I wanted him dead, and he hasn't done anything to me like he's done to you." She grabbed his arms. "Wolfman, you didn't kill him. You've just prevented him from killing thousands, maybe millions of people. I still think you were a wipe to come here alone — but so was I."

His gaze unfocused. "But you don't know how close it was, Andy. How can I ever trust myself? What if it happens again?"

Andrea thought for a moment. "Well, in the first place, Tram's a sociopath. Other people aren't even real to him. He thinks he's the only being in the universe, and the rest of us are like little toy soldiers to play with. And in the second place," her gaze sharpened on him, "you did control it. I doubt you'll ever be in a situation more likely to make you lose control. If you didn't turn rogue just now, you're not going to do it tomorrow over something less important."

The Shenn rolled up and touched his arm with its optic fibers. Jason looked at it thoughtfully, then nodded.

"Sssrei says I've finished with Trammerden," he told Andrea. "I've broken the enemy-bond and put a stop to his plans." He stroked the Shenn's body with a little smile. "Sssrei tells me it's time to forget about Tram and think about my own future."

"Perceptive friend you have there."

"Yeah." He drew a long, deep breath and

rested his elbows on his knees, then looked at her sideways. "You came after me," he said. It was almost a question.

Andrea looked down at her hands. She was nervous. "I was pretty annoyed with you," she said. "And I finally figured out why." Andrea reached out and took his hand; she could not bring herself to meet his eyes. "I'm not much good at this," she said and glanced briefly at him. He was silent, but the question was still in his eyes. She took another breath and started over.

"I've fought so hard. For so long. I've lost a lot of friends — simply because I've gone for what I wanted, instead of making excuses. And because I'm good. So." She shrugged. "I'm careful. Even with Victoria and Weasel. I see the resentment in their eyes sometimes, and it hurts. But not enough to stop me — only enough to make me cautious. It drives Vic and Weasel crazy, sometimes." Then she met his gaze. "I guess somewhere along the way I started to trust you, MacLeod. And love you. I. . . ." Andrea finished in a whisper, "I wasn't going to let Trammerden take that away from me. I won't let anyone, anyone but you, take you away from me."

Jason pulled her to him. She buried her face in his hair; tears rolled from her eyes. She held him, and he her, for a long moment.

They drew apart and smiled at each other, a little embarrassed. Then Andrea slapped her thighs and stood.

"Come on. We've got to figure out how to lift the comm blackout before those drones reach Ceres."

They shut off the maze's grav generator from the same terminal Jason had used earlier. Then they threaded their way through the deadly mirror maze to the command center.

Getting into the system turned out to be easy. Although Trammerden's command center was defended with many barriers and death traps, he had only given his programming a simple password. Since the command center terminals were the only access to his secret programs, it had no doubt seemed safe enough. And he was already logged in. Jason sat down at the console and got to work.

Andrea watched while Jason tracked Trammerden's files and commands. In moments he looked up, flushed with excitement.

"Look." Above the holo-table, three ships appeared. The perspective of the hologram was that of the lead ship. In the distance, one asteroid stood out, a drifting star much brighter than the ones that surrounded it. Ceres.

"The drones. ETA sixty-four minutes." He typed in a swift command. Andrea gave Jason a curious glance.

"Wait," he said. "It'll take several minutes for the command to reach the drones."

Andrea held her breath. Moments passed. Abruptly the hologram dissolved in a blinding flash.

"I detonated the bomb," he said, grinning.

Andrea whooped. He shot to his feet and hugged Andrea, lifted her off the ground, and swung her in a circle. His green eyes were shining.

"Let's lift the blackout and contact the others," Andrea said. "Are they ever going to be surprised!"

Jason lay on a cushion in the rec center, chin on his bandaged hands, staring out at the stars. He was waiting for Andrea. Behind him, Weasel, François, and Nöel had the thrideo tuned to the news, awaiting the latest word from the peace conference. Sssrei was in the reactor chamber, soaking up a much-needed meal of electromagnetism.

It had been two days since Jason and Andrea had returned with Trammerden. Classes had not resumed yet, but things were slowly returning to normal. Trammerden was locked up, and the admin staff and professors had been released — after a series of psych tests verified what Trammerden had told Jason: Tram had worked alone, without accomplices.

That morning, Jason and Andrea had spent hours in a tolyernet conference with the Collegium Council. The memory brought a grimace to his face; that old Darenkov was a real shark.

The seven-member Council had listened to Jason's description of the convolver, and the Shenns' needs, in attentive silence. They were holographic ghosts who stared at Andrea and Jason in turn.

Darenkov was the worst. She had eyed Jason

severely as he related what he had done. Her small eyes, pale blue and buried in wrinkles, glittered like chips of ice. Now she spoke with deliberate, glacial slowness.

"You're saying that they are offering to give us this dimensional shift field and all they want in return is a bionics factory?"

Jason nodded. "The convolver has very little use to them, under the circumstances. They had conceived of it but they couldn't build it; faster-than-light travel was only a theory until Sssrei and I put the convolver together. Without 'companions' they're as helpless as newborns. And a lot more fragile."

One of the other members, a retired admiral from the first Mars colony, spoke.

"Then how have they survived and developed this civilization you describe? You make them sound as if they're on the verge of extinction, but they seemed to have done all right for themselves. . . ."

Jason's brow knit. "No. They used to have a telepathic relationship with another silicone species on 40 Eridani II; they called them the Aabssa. The Aabssa weren't intelligent — they had no more thinking capacity than an insect, but they were larger and a lot more durable and mobile than the Shenn. The two races had sort of evolved together."

The admiral's beetle eyebrows went up. "A symbiosis."

"Exactly." Jason hesitated. "After it was removed from its birth pool, a Shenn infant would adopt an Aabssa larva. It was placed in a cavity in the Aabssa's body and bonded with it telepathically and, as they grew older, also physically. By the time they were adults, there was no way to physically separate the two. They became a single unit."

Borrowed memories flooded Jason's thoughts: the race memories he had shared with Sssrei of the slow melding that had occurred between the two species. Of the transparent, spiderlike ShennAabssa; the crystalline cities; the sundrink festivals; rainbow reflections from a million oiled surfaces....

"This was a long time ago," Jason added. "They called themselves the ShennAabssa, then." He paused. "That was when they developed their civilization, their technology and mathematics. Different from ours, maybe not quite as advanced as we are right now, in some ways. In other ways, far more advanced."

"What happened to the Aabssa?" one of the other councilmembers asked.

"There was a plague. It wiped out the Aabssa, utterly, and the Shenn who were in symbiosis with them. The only ones left were the infants who hadn't bonded yet, and the very old whose Aabssa companions died of old age and liquified before the plague."

He frowned and looked around at the silent Council.

"Anyhow," he said, "the Shenn, what's left of them, have been hiding in the caves of 40 Eridani II for — I figure it's been close to a thousand years. They had all the time they wanted to expand their knowledge. Their minds work differently from ours; they have a better grasp of other dimensions. Sssrei's been pretty careful to shield that part of his mind from me, but I've caught a couple of glimpses. . . ." He shrugged and refocused his thoughts. Darenkov's stare was making him nervous.

"Their numbers have dwindled," he said. "They're extremely fragile, physically, and there are predators on Shenndri that are immune to their telepathy. Instantaneous space travel doesn't do them any good at all if they can't even go outside to eat without endangering their lives."

He leaned forward. "They can help us, Colleagues. And we can help them."

They had given him no answer then, but had insisted on questioning Andrea, and then had sent them both away. Andrea had predicted privately that it would be some time before they knew what the Council's decision would be.

Jason had been a nervous wreck for the last several hours. The Council still had not contacted them.

"Hey, compadre! Look. They're talking about us."

He twisted; Weasel was pointing at the thrideo. A newscaster was talking.

". . . Collegium, where, according to our sources, a small group of dedicated cadets has taken over the school and prevented the deaths of thousands — including the peace delegations from all over the solar system."

Jason came over and sat down in front of the

thrideo. Victoria, Thomas, and some others came in, laughing; they were peremptorily silenced. Everyone gathered around.

The newscaster continued to relate the story of what had happened at Collegium for the benefit of billions of people all over the solar system. Other than a few mispronounced names and minor inaccuracies, he got the story pretty much right. They even used photos of the principals in the action: Victoria, Weasel, Thomas, Simon, Andrea. The students laughed and nudged each other. Then they displayed a shot of Jason from his first Collegium days and a horribly inaccurate sketch of Sssrei.

"And the two most unusual heroes," the newscaster was saying. "The one on the right is Jason MacLeod, whom the Collegium Council has retroactively named valedictorian of the Collegium class of 2087." Victoria, Weasel, and Thomas grinned at him — color flooded into his face; his mouth fell open. "The title belonged formerly," the newscaster added, "to Jon Trammerden, who has been formally charged with murder, attempted murder, conspiracy, and high treason — other charges are pending on further investigation. . . .

"And on the left, an artist's conception of the sole ambassador to the human race of a sentient alien race on 40 Eridani II." The newscaster's face grew large as the cam-I's panned close.

"Peaceful contact has been made with an alien species, the Shenn," he said. Jason could not repress a smile at the solemn, important tone of the man's voice. It was too bad Sssrei was not there to experience it.

"As a result of this historic event, representatives from the Trans-Martian Commonwealth and the Earth Aggregate peace delegations have quickly settled on a tentative agreement and are on their way to Collegium to meet with the Shenn ambassador. Your newscaster will be on the spot, with updates as they occur. . . ."

The others slapped Jason on the back. Everyone was talking at once. Jason smiled dazedly and nodded vague acknowledgement of their congratulations. Then, suddenly, he jumped to his feet with a hoot of delight; the others looked at him, surprised. He did not bother to explain; he merely ran out the door. He had to find Sssrei and Andrea.

The Council had released the whole, true story to the news media. Sssrei's people would have their companions — and deep space exploration was about to undergo a dramatic revolution. Things were about to start happening, fast and furious.

Jason stopped in the reaction chamber only long enough to pick up Sssrei. He shook his head, grinning, at the alien's repeated demands for enlightenment and raced through the corridors to the medical module.

Andrea was in the med center, by Cmdr. Turin's life support unit. A mini-thrideo had been set up to one side of the unit. Andrea broke into a smile when Jason dashed into the room.

"Hey, hero. You're looking a bit disheveled."

She nodded toward Turin. "I was just filling Linc in on some of the details the newscast left out."

Jason came up beside her. Turin was conscious; his eyes focused on Jason. His body was smeared with violet gel, and he hung suspended in a null-grav sterile field that shimmered about him like a faint aurora borealis.

"MacLeod." Turin's voice was a weedy whisper. "I remember you from before." His gaze lighted on Sssrei. "Please extend greetings to the ambassador for me."

Jason exchanged a look, eye to fiber, with Sssrei.

"Sssrei asks me to convey its appreciation for your attempt to stop Trammerden," he said.

Turin drew a careful breath. "Heard about the Council's decision. Congratulations. Thought you should've been valley all along."

Jason nodded. He could not suppress a smile of pleasure. Then he sobered. "Sorry you got caught in the middle, Commander."

Turin shook his head. "Little regen and I'll be fine. Only lost a few vital organs. . . ." His chuckle turned into a cough. Andrea stood and blew him a kiss.

"We'll let you rest, Linc. I'll see you before they ship you out tomorrow."

Jason preceded Andrea into the hall.

"He going to be okay?"

Andrea nodded, dark eyes smiling. "Dr. Talies says he'll be good as new in a few months. Now, come on." She punched him in the arm. "What's the big news?"

Jason leaned against the corridor wall. "You know, Andy, I've been thinking. When I sell my first convolution field generator, I'll come into a lot of money."

"True," Andrea said. She propped herself against the wall beside him and put her hands into her pockets, eyeing him.

"So it occurred to me. Why not invest part of the money in my own exsol cruiser and fit it with a convolver?"

A tentative light had come into her eyes. But she merely nodded soberly. Jason looked at her. A powerful emotion squeezed his heart.

"Anyhow," he said, in an off-handed tone, "once things are under way to get the Shenn companions built, I won't need to stick around any more. I don't want to be an executive. I want to go exploring — start an exsol company of my own. I'll need partners who know about outsystem exploration. And I'll need friends around me, people I know I can trust."

"You mean Linc?"

Jason burst out laughing and hugged her. "I mean you, idiot! You weren't kidding when you said you were too slagging careful." Then he grew serious and released her. "So what about it, Colleague? You want to be a business partner?"

She frowned and looked away. "Jason, you shouldn't be so hasty. I mean, we might end up not being able to stand each other. You're talking about a lot of money, a major investment. I have nothing to contribute."

Jason gave her a sardonic look. "Don't be

ridiculous. You have your piloting skills — which, I might add, are formidable. And you already have a background in xenogeology.

"Look, Andy," he said, "I'm going to have more money than I'll know what to do with. Sssrei will be an invisible partner; I'm going to split the profits evenly between his factory and my exsol company. And you're just as responsible for things working out as Sssrei and I are — if you hadn't aborted the exercise, Trammerden would have succeeded. I couldn't have done it without you, Ito. You have a right to be in on this. If you want to be."

She looked at him with a sidelong glance. There were tears in her eyes, but she was smiling. "You serious?"

"No, I'm tormenting you just to be cruel. Of course I'm serious."

"In that case, Colleague," she said, "you've got yourself a partner."

Jason stuck out his hand. They shook on it, grinning idiotically at each other. Sssrei wrapped its own filaments about their handclasp.

"I must tell those of my pooling," Sssrei thought to Jason, enthusiastic. "I have entered into a human-style business transaction."

Jason grabbed Andrea's hand and picked Sssrei up. "Come on, let's go for a spin, before the reporters track onto us. How about Arcturus? Or the Pleiades? You name it."

Andrea threw her arms about his neck. He wrapped his arms about her waist. They smiled into each other's eyes. "I've got an even better idea," she said. "Let's sneak back to Europa. I want to show you my hometown. We'll dress up like jAggs so no one will recognize us. Have you ever been to Forty Leagues About?" Jason shook his head. "Dull, dull, dull," she assured him. "But it'll be fun to go there as tourists."

Sssrei interrupted with high excitement. "May we return to Shenndri for a short time, also? I'd like to inform my people. They've waited so long . . . I want them to know."

They started down the hall, together, the three of them: pilot, alien, renegade. Jason laughed.

"Easy," he said. "We have all the time in the world."